The Man with the White Hat and Other Stories

The Man with the White Hat and Other Stories

Uvie Ann-Marie Giwewhegbe

malthouse

Malthouse Press Limited

Lagos, Benin, Ibadan, Jos, Port-Harcourt, Zaria

© Uvie Ann-Marie Giwewhegbe 2017
First Published 2017
ISBN: 978-978-540-707-5

Published and manufactured in Nigeria by

Malthouse Press Limited
43 Onitana Street, Off Stadium Hotel Road,
Off Western Avenue, Lagos Mainland
E-mail: malthouse_press@yahoo.com
malthouselagos@gmail.com
Website: malthouselagos.com
Tel: +234 802 600 3203

Dedication

To God Almighty, my help.
My family who are my consistent friends and encouraged me
in every way, especially my mother, Mrs Magdalene
Giwewhegbe; she gave me stories.

The Stories

Jumai

Jumai was only twelve when she was told she was ripe for marriage. Her parents reminded her that it was traditional for her to be married and, by this time, bearing children.

What was she to know about child bearing? Her teacher, Aunty Mimi, had talked on this issue in class when she discussed the topic "sex education". She emphasized how important it was to abstain until marriage and how early marriage, especially for under-age girls, comes with diseases such as Vesico Vaginal Fistula (VVF), cancer, infections, mental cases and yes...pain, intense pain, especially when pregnant or during delivery. Jumai was lost in thought and confusion, all she wanted was to be a girl, an achiever, but she was too young to say "no" to her parents who have emphasized demands of their religion.

The day of her marriage came, Jumai sat under a tree behind her house when her best friend Amina came to visit.

"Jumai," Amina said thinking of a way to console her friend, 'it's not the end of the world you know, tears won't bring a solution."

Jumai sat in silence as the tears increased and waited for her name to be called to see her groom.

"Jumai!" screamed her mother, heartily.

Jumai hesitantly walked to the house, her heart almost tore out of her chest when she was introduced to her groom.

1

A stout dark old man, that stared as she walked in with his bulgy eyes. His smiles expressed his gladness and fulfillment. All that danced in his mind was "I have found a fine fish."

Poor Jumai she only wondered how she will fare as a fifth wife; bear children and raise a home, what did she know?

The old man she was told to call 'Gwarzo', now her husband, meaning "man above man" picked his bride and Jumai left her parent's home without looking back to say good bye to her family as she walked away soaked in pain and worry.

****

Gwarzo's house was a two bedroom flat with little space. The living-room had paraphernalia of carved wood on his shelf of different animals and tools. It was dark with no ventilation and she was welcomed by four huge women with ten children. Obviously, the women were Gwarzo's wives and the children were his. She wondered where they all slept and how they coped, even when their names were called and they were being introduced, she could not recall a single name except for her contemporary, Uzi, who was the second child of the second wife and also the only female amongst her children. She felt consoled, she had a peer. Uzi looked so lonely and timid, but that did not deter Jumai.

Night came, and then she knew how they all slept. The children slept in the living room, the wives in a small room and Gwarzo had the large room to himself. Jumai was fed and given water to bath. As soon as she finished, the first wife, who seemed friendly, gave her a pair of cotton clothing and guided her to Gwarzo's room, after which she said "massage his back, he likes it."

Jumai walked into the room, with candle lights all over and a naked hairy man awaiting her arrival. He tapped the bed thrice and smiled while he motioned for her to come to bed. She shivered, wondering her experience. And then as she walked toward the bed hesitantly and sat by the side, he drew her close and whispered in her eyes "my darling, you will love me." Jumai was drowned in disgust as he slowly laid her down, taking off her clothing and all everyone could hear was a scream.

"You are a sweet virgin," Gwarzo said, every night he had sex with Jumai it was continuous, and the poor girl was sinking in pain and repelled by his ways.

Months passed, and it took the first wife to notice Jumai was pregnant. The constant nausea and morning sickness, she spat on wherever she stepped.

"Jumai," called the first wife seated outside when Jumai was spitting away, "come my dear. *Aban godiya ne a sami rai a cikin rai*. You are pregnant my dear and the joy of motherhood is primary."

Jumai stood bewildered at what the first wife had said. Her heart skipped a beat when she realized she might be right. Her eyes weighed so heavy with tears and her lips could not voice her pain. She quickly ran to the room reserved for the wives. The tears rolled when she figured she will be a mother, a child a mother, then, the words of Aunty Mimi began to replay in her mind "it's like a child catering for a child. What is there to gain?"

****

Nine months passed so quickly with less food and nourishment. There was no mercy in chores or responsibility especially in massaging Gwarzo. The man had a way of making his request "pregnancy or no pregnancy! Jumai's soft hands will rest my shoulders" he says patronizing her.

Jumai in her tiny frame, lifting weight in malnourishment, lacking every necessary attention until the D-day arrived. The house wives hurdled around the house preparing hot water and searching for the wrapper they usually use in wrapping the child after birth, a wrapper never washed.

"Push! Push!" they kept screaming into Jumai's ears. She used all the energy she could afford while in pain and wondering if this was her last. The tear stringed and then, she heard a cry, a loud cry after five straight hours of force, pain and energy. Jumai sealed her eyes in relief when she felt it was over while the house wives wrapped the baby in an unclean wrapper. The second wife lifted the child and said "Amarya, it's a girl." Jumai did not open her eyes but nodded in reception. The third wife picked a rusty metal that laid beside them and cut the umbilical cord.

The baby was so skinny and malnourished. Jumai called her Latifah. Food was barely enough for the entire family, talk more of an additional member and a lactating mother, left alone to cater for it. And so it was no surprise when Latifah died prematurely three weeks after her birth while her mother was left to nurse emotional and physical pains. At this moment, Uzi was her consolation.

Jumai and Uzi became quite friendly. They did most of the chores together and shared their secrets. On one of their moments together, Jumai said to her "Uzi, I am so sad. I want to die!"

"No, No…" Uzi said, "Please, don't think like that. Do you want the truth? I despise my father. His ways annoy me."

She sighs and continues.

"He said I should not school because…because I am a woman. That he will marry me off soon. I always envy children I see going to school, wearing their uniforms, looking smart and serious."

Uzi sounded depressed while Jumai stared in pity.

"Hmmm…" said Jumai, "what do we do?"

Uzi gazed into the sun and blinked when she could not retain the rays and said "kill the pain… and sadness."

Jumai was not certain about what Uzi meant but she picked what she understood, she only wondered if she had the courage to handle it. By this time, Jumai had already started encountering pain around her abdomen, constant urination and she smelt putrid.

On that night, one of Gwarzo's special requests for Jumia, Jumai held a rusty nail she had found earlier on in the day.

Gwarzo slowly undressed her as usual and crooned "my Amarya… if no you, no life," he chuckled "massage me small."

His request for a massage seemed so convenient and the situation seemed perfect. But then, as she hopped on his back, Gwarzo could not help himself in his irritation when he perceived the stench that surrounded her.

"Jumai! You smell like a dead rat! *Mai ya faru?*" he put his hand to his nose.

The poor girl had no response but drowned in self-pity when she remembered how the wives closed their nostrils and the little children in the house mocked her earlier in the day. She wondered what was wrong and she could not decipher. But, at that moment she knew Gwarzo had triggered her emotions enough for her to be courageous to exert her aim.

As she massaged him she said "Gwarzo?" speaking softly.

"uhmmm…" he replied, taking pleasure in the gesture, forgetting the stench and not acknowledging the profundity in her voice.

"I…. I want a divorce," she stammered.

Suddenly, his eyes waved open, perplexed at how audacious and unconsciously he yelled "what?!"

"I don't want this marriage anymore!" she opened up courageously.

Gwarzo pushed her away and rose from the bed looking sternly into her eyes and slapped her thrice. He called her ungrateful and a whore. He asks her if she had another lover and she denied it. He beat her mercilessly.

"I will teach you a lesson!" he said, he grabs her and pushes her to the bed, and quickly takes his trousers off. He hops on her and while he struggled with her to fit himself in, she remembers the nail in her hand and stabs him in the eye.

The pain was electrifying as he screams almost losing his breath. This wakes everyone in the house.

"Ayaya…" he kept saying as though it killed the pain.

Jumai quickly ran out of the room and of the house. She kept running until she could not feel her feet and she was a distance away. Her pains were intense, coupled with the beating she just had. She continued to run in exhaustion, passing through a bush path without turning back.

She slowly began to lose her breath and the pain was making her weak, very weak. Then, she saw a reflection of light on a lonely path, as she walked ahead and when she looked up, she saw a tall building and on it was written "St. Gabriel's Orphanage." She smiled, but she was too weak to proceed. And so she dragged her feet till she began to crawl, then she found herself at the foot of the building where she collapsed under the lights.

Suddenly, she heard a voice, a sweet voice whisper and say "You are home," and that was when she smiled after one year of torture.

The Man with the White Hat

I saw him daily. Every time. I see him on my way to school or late in the evenings when I am helping my mother sell groceries. The man with the white hat and the firm walking stick...the hat is never off, neither is it tainted or stained, always pure white.

He was a man of his early sixties, trailing the street through and fro, morning till evening. He is either speaking to himself or pointing his firm stick at one situation or another. I wondered if he even had a family. I called him the "classy mad" since he always wore clean clothes and his hat was ever white, but my perception changed on this very day I am about to reveal.

My name is Uya, a twelve-year old with a hunger for adventure. I am from a village called Pan which is civilized with no neglect for tradition and culture. My father died when I was seven when he went hunting. According to my mother, he was the best hunter alive but he was killed by what he hunted, a bull. Legend has it that I am from an ancestry of hunters and spiritualists. Once I was told that my paternal greatest grandfather who died known as the greatest spiritualist ever known to Pan, cursed a spirit world for reasons unknown. This was one out of many that fed my curiosity as a twelve year old with an interest for history and the arts. My mother used to accuse me of stealing little artefacts whenever we visit the museum when I was between the age of seven and eight. It therefore should not surprise anyone when I got interested in this old mad whom I consider crazy with class. I observed that he was always pointing at a particular direction with his walking stick whenever he passes by and then he'll shake his head. All the women on the street have a way of laughing at him whenever he does that or they gossip and say things like "that hat no dey comot?"

One of those days on my way back from school, at noon, I decided to follow a bush part to ease myself after which I will take the main road. I saw him squeeze himself into a hole. I was intrigued but yet shocked and frightened. I reckon I take a sneak-peak but the courage was absent. I inhaled and exhaled, bracing myself and summoning courage, when I was sure I had the brevity, I walked towards the hole. It was so tiny. I wondered how he went through. It was surrounded by branches and leaves of a rare kind. Before I could think of how to go through the hole, I figured running was a better option.

As I lay on my bed, tossing and turning, all I thought of was if the man with the white hat was even human. The number of thoughts that infringed my mind was like a web with no head-way. My mother observed how weird I was that evening...am sure she thought I was on my period or probably I had a fight in school. She asked me several questions that all I can remember saying was "nothing".

I hate to bother my mother. She is overwhelmed with looking after me and baring the thoughts of being a widow. She always has a way of reminding one of my Father's absence, especially in her looks. I certainly could not burden her with suspicion and so I decided to keep my strange observation to myself and dig for a revelation.

I timed him again, taking the bush path at noon, and I was not late. With my heart in my throat, hiding behind a tree, I saw him look left and right and then he squeezed himself into the whole. I reckoned I have to sit and wait for him to come out, and I did. I remember playing with a leaf as I waited and then I slept off. I felt a sudden chill and that was when I opened my eyes. It was dark and I was lying on a bed of leaves. In fear and surprise, I peeped to see if the man with the white hat was out when I saw no sign of him, I took to my heels.

My mother was upset. I do not remember the last time I made her that angry. She nagged about my being home late and vowed to punish me the next time I did so again. I feared the warning or admonition but it was not enough to allay my curiosity.

The next day, on my way back from school, I decided to take the bush path again but I was distracted by my friend, Tobi, who said there was a party along the road and we had to go eat some free food. How could I reject free food? I followed her to the party and realized it was a funeral of an old hunter in the village. The event was so dramatic, with hunters of his age-group displaying bows and arrows while they danced in circles. It was a tradition to recognize every hunter in death, specially for their skills in hunting and their techniques in it. The entire village acknowledges them as warriors but of animals. Although I see no reason for them to be revered since whatever they hunt is being sold to us...but who am I to counter existing tradition.

The event had not drawn away my curiosity. In fact, the free food I was hoping to consume was not available, not even the free meat everyone was entitled to got to me. I was furious with myself, wondering why I had not followed my intuition to obey my curiosity. Before darkness started crawling in, I virtually tip-toed away from the event. Tobi was too engrossed to notice. I ran along the way all to ensure I meet up with the man with the white hat. My school bag weighed on me as I ran into the bush. I headed straight for the hole and I was perturbed with what I saw. I saw nothing! I was confused as I tried retracing my steps from the previous days and wondered if I took the right route to get to the hole, but, there was nothing wrong with my geography. The hole in the rock had disappeared.

Darkness was setting in. I walked home disappointed, dragging my bag as I walked. I knocked on my door but my mother was not home. That was an added fury to my system. As I sat by my doorstep waiting on my Mother, I wondered what kind of sorcery could this be? Or was I hallucinating? Then am thankful I told no one or they may tag me mad too. My mother arrived before I could question my thoughts. She embraced me, acknowledging how tired and angry I must be. If only she knew I felt worse.

The next day was a Saturday. I had the luxury of waking when I choose to but considerate enough to follow my mother to the market to sell her goods. I was deep in sleep, lying like a log, when suddenly I heard voices, voices I was sure were in my dream. The voices were getting louder and familiar. Dazed with sleep, I opened my eyes and realized I was not dreaming, my mother and someone were having a conversation. I walked to the living-room to see who it was and my heart could not take it. It was the man with the white hat sipping water from our cup, speaking like a normal human and my mother seemed to be enjoying his company. Before I could run away, my mother called out to me.

"Uya! Don't run away...we have a guest."

That was when he turned around. He was a fine young man with glazed eyes, a toned skin and a flashy smile.

"Hello Uya...it's a pleasure."

I woke up wet on my bed, seems buckets of water were being poured on me and I was surrounded by a group of women trying to console my mother. She was crying out loud until they told her I was awake. Tears of Joy flowed this time. I asked her what had happened and she said I fainted as soon as I saw the man with the white hat.

"Uya, you have been off for two hours...were you so shocked from seeing such a handsome man with your mother?"

"No mother," I said, "but...what is his name? And, is he gone?"

"Yes my dear..." she said. "His name is Till and he left but will be back tomorrow."

It was that minute I knew my life was about to change. I did not even feel my mother's caress.

I will be a liar if I say I did not anticipate his coming. There were moments I actually turned to my mother to ask her if Till was ever going to come again. It has been two weeks since he visited my home and every day I wake my heart hangs in my throat with thoughts that I may see him but he did not return. One night, when my mother had to pursue an errand and left me home alone, I thought I could sit by my window and gaze at the beautiful constellation of stars that I had seen, listening to the crickets chirping and the sheep at a neighbour's bleating, someone now said, "it's all so beautiful, isn't it?". Before I could think of replying, I wondered if I was hallucinating. My neck became so stiff; turning around to search for the voice was not a plan. Gently, I turned and there he was, the man with the white hat seated with his legs crossed on my bed. He looked so magnificent and harmless, dressed in white. He certainly was not the old man I had seen at first but the handsome young man I fainted for.

"Hello Uya!" he said, with his glazed eyes staring at me. "I know you have been following me and I do not blame you but your curiosity. And I resent that."

When he said that my smile went upside down and then I was overwhelmed with fear.

"But Uya," he continued, "I will feed your curiosity. I will be here, as late, as soon as you hear a neigh, you will jump over your window. Am I clear?"

I nodded.

"Good bye then," and he disappeared. It was then I realized I had not said a word.

Morning came. I have never looked forward to a new day but this one. The thought of hearing a house neigh made me truly excited, felt magical. I was full of smiles the entire day. My mother wondered what the excitement was all about but, I couldn't tell, made it feel like a lifetime secret. When evening came, I deliberately avoided a conversation with my mother. I ran to my room at the specified time. I could not close my eyes in anticipation. I waited and waited, realizing the time was way past and the minute my eye lids were about to seal in disappointment, I heard the horse neigh. In excitement I looked out my window and I saw the most beautiful memory I have always cherished till this moment. I have never seen a reflection so pure, glittery white with Till on it, smiling while I rushed out. The horse was so restless braising its hooves on the ground, neighing loud. I thought the neighbours would awaken but the man with the white hat assured me that no one could hear us. He sounded like a god. He lifted me on the horse and took me on a journey of light. A horse with so much speed and power, I did not know when we had reached our destination.

We halted in front of a wall covered with green climbers. When we alighted from the horse, Till went for the wall placing his right palm on it while he used his left to dismiss the horse, waving as a signal. The horse disappeared like a sparse of glitters. I was awed and speechless, almost deaf to the man with the white hat when he said "let's go!" We passed through a thin passage covered with climbers as though they were the frame of the wall. The walk was long as we kept taking corners until we got to a wide silver gate, he dusted his feet by the gate and motioned I do the same which I did, and then the gate opened. I have never seen a place look so pure. The grasses and trees were so green and alive with owls of different colours cooing and flying pass. There were no other animals that I know of cause all I saw were owls, large in size, louder than a saxophone but I have never seen a place look so green and pure, with a smell of freshness and the ground felt so soft. Till was ahead of me observing absolute silence as we walked pass not taking note of how bedazzled I was. The sky glowed making the environment look so loveable. Then I started seeing thatched huts as we passed and then people. These were not ordinary people my heart rested in my throat as I was terrified with the sight, forgetting my previous memories. They were all one eyed, with their hands looking scaly and their feet were large looking like that of a duck, they stared keenly as we passed, I could swear I was dinner. As we walked passed climbing down a stairs moulded with rocks, I saw what looked like a shed surrounded by green climbers but it had a shape of a circle with a man in it giving what looked like a tiny bottle to a queue of people each waiting to be attended to, in exchange for something wrapped in a tiny white cloth. They all looked so sick and grotesque. I observed there were no children around and it was then I was certain I could be dinner.

As we approached a very large tree we passed through gigantic armed men, with two eyes this time holding on to their spears obviously taller than they are. They stood in array on both sides and they were uncountable and unshaken. I felt so tired walking towards the large tree, the movement felt endless. And then, we halted in front of a thatched hut surrounded with lit candles and I heard humming which sounded like a group with different tunes to it. Till and I entered the hut and true to my suspicion there were seven women, all two eyed, humming in a synchronized tune to appease someone and when we drew close I saw it was their King. A midget, fair complexioned and sick. I will never forget the way he smiled at me, so cheerful despite his state. I was frightened but I smiled back, wondering how he was coping coughing non-stop and it seemed as though the humming calmed him.

"You are welcome my dear to Hirma spirit world," he smiled while he coughed. "The one we seek, the true descent. Till, you have done well."

He stammered while withholding the cough.

Till knelt in obeisance while I being the child I was and extremely frightened I followed. It seemed the King observed my fear.

"Sweet girl, I am King Nagumbe of Hirma and I am aware that your name is Uya."

He then smiled.

"You are safe. We seek not to destroy you but for you to liberate us. Please, one of you *Ufas* should offer her a drink. A welcome one" he insisted.

Apparently, females were not females but *Ufas*, I was marvelled.

The drink came…"yulk!" I don't even remember the colour but I remember keeping it aside and sitting mute. What baffled me though was the sudden silence Till wore on his face with a sign of regret. He sat beside me still kneeling but in spite of silence I suddenly felt at ease.

The king then arrange for a bonfire and dancing. We all sat by a heap of woods stacked on fire while some *ufas* danced around it screaming happily with drummers providing rhythm with the accord of sticks and funny whistling. It was all so fun, even Till's spirit was also lifted. The king wore a smile all through and he coughed while he did. I remember him looking so pitiful as though he would die every time he coughed. The community was no different as many drowned their pains just to enjoy that moment. I wondered what was going on.

The next day, with all hung over from the previous day's activity, I was presented before the King once more whom I now say in a serious state despite his persistent cough with blood. I pitied him, but I was helpless to his cause...or so I thought. He asked that we should be left alone and requested for Till's presence whom suddenly appeared in a split second sitting beside the King. The King's eyes rested on me as though he was searching for words, then, he began to tell me a story, it sounded so much so.

"Your ancestry is known for hunting and conversing with the gods. They hunted the best and the gods obeyed all they said and answered all their requests," he stammered, coughing intensely at intervals as he spoke. "In the days of old, one of your ancestors, Budinme the great they called him. Blessed and cursed with the presence of the gods. He was your great grandfather which I'm sure you never met. You see, that myth about a cursed spirit world is true and that cursed spirit world is us."

The words he spoke were so slow and I felt his pain and regret.

"My child," he continued, "Budinme was a man of wrath, with was his curse. His mind was always blinded by his certainty of being favoured by the gods and so he blessed and cursed as he pleased. His anger was doubled when his wife, Irima, a beautiful damsel whom he seized from his King Bako, because he had the power to, was cheating on him with a man from this spirit world. I have never seen love so pure but Budinme saw it as war. Blamed my world for permitting such and I was very unaware, surprised when I learnt. Budinme gave no time for pardon or mercy, we don't know his communication with the gods but the next day the entire Hirma was surrounded by pain. All were coughing out blood, some were maimed instantly by it. That's why you see some of us one-eyed and others so frail. We are not mortals my child, and so we live and not die cause our existence is in nature but I tell you, I would take up mortality to end this ever long pain upon myself and my people."

It all sounded like one of the stories told in school by my teacher except it felt real. I was overwhelmed while he spoke, his difficulty in speech and his obvious pain which was everywhere. All I could hear at the background was groaning, moaning of pain. Till on the other hand was seated on the floor with his head bowed down and his hat in his hand and it was at that moment I observed he was the only healthy spirit. I could not question that but I heard something new while the King spoke.

"My child, we beseech you to intercede for us. Your grandfather cannot be reached because he is bound in chains eternally and surrounded by lions with seven heads against anyone who tries to save him which I would not suggest. However, there is this staff of his buried under your house. The staff has been mystified that only the blood of a descent can make it whole and you, my child, is one out of many descents with sincere purity and strong will. That's why we chose you."

By this time, I was confused and frightened wondering if I was on a suicide mission.

"Till will come with you," he said, "you must be on the journey, my people are in pain," placing his hand on my shoulder made me feel like a soldier.

The King whispered some few words to Till, while certain *Ufas* were fetching some weapons which from the story

18

narrated, I thought we may not need. And then they brought transportation, the white horse that brought me to Hirma, which I was delighted to see and a black horse for Till. I wonder if I was being sympathetic or childish because I felt no responsibility towards these spirits, but then, I saw a spirit fading in pain not too far from the King's stead and then I knew I was responsible.

Our journey began immediately. My zest for adventure and deep curious nature blinded me to what was ahead. The minute we walked out of Hirma I felt the sun, it lit up my skin like fire. We walked through the bush paths where I observed Till, just there were no humans on sight. I asked Till why I could not see a human given the time of the day.

"You are in a form we call *Taluma*. You cannot see because this path you think you know is not what you know. This is the spirit version."

He sighs.

"I brought this upon my people Uya," he said that with deep pain, sorrow and regret while he bowed his head.

"What do you mean?" I asked trying to hold the horse steady after we heard a howl.

"I questioned my King so much, about the human race and why they could not see us but we them, he said we all had a purpose and place and certain answers can't be given. I was so young and bored."

He chuckles in tears.

"One day, I heard certain spirits speak of a spirit who once turned human just to taste their food. The spirit was Shoba, an *Ufa* known to be adventurous which displeased many and made her outcast. I went to her late one night and she told me how she did it. She called it her experiment."

19

His eyes lit up with memories he never forgot, and he continued.

"She blew what looked like powder to my face and suddenly I felt a difference after which she reserved some in a little sack and handed it to me saying if I needed to return all I had to do was rub it on my face. She then showed me a path in-between a tree which I took and it led me to the human world. I never felt so alive, Uya, especially after I saw her. She was so beautiful. I met her on the bush part fetching firewood. We fell in love at first sight, a feeling I had never known. It made my chest hurt and jump but yet I wore a very loud smile. "Irima" he exhaled after her name, while I was full of surprise. We met in secret, and I did not return home because of her. She then told me she was married to a spiritualist whom every world feared, Burdinme. I was not scared, I was ready to die for love until one day he caught us under a tree, kissing, I knew my life was over and I never saw it fit to beg. Irima knelt, pleading to her husband to forgive us and I did not budge, I was consumed with so much pride and the need to defend my love. I think I scoffed at him while he fumed in anger. He asked where I was from, and I was stupid enough to reveal. Then he walked away after spitting at my feet. I returned to the tree where I always slept and decided to check on Irima in the morning. I woke up with her corpse hanging above my head. I assure you, Uya, I have not known joy or peace since that day. And when I returned home, I saw my people in a plague of pain, my King said my curious nature was my curse, a curse I laid upon them all. By time I felt it dim to apologize to Burdinme, I learnt a lioness hunted him down.

Poor guy, I thought, no wonder he is ready for any risk just to redeem himself. He must have been burdened for too long, I just prayed I could help as they said I would.

The howl became louder as we basked in the moment. The horse halted immediately and neighed in fear and then from nowhere wolves came from between the trees. Seven different wolves with three heads each, gnashing their teeth and growling. I was so terrified, never had I seen something so hideous. Till, in expectation, called them "the woxers" guards of evil. I wanted to run when Till valiantly rushed them, slitting their throats with a sword with so much speed. I could not just sit on the horse and stare especially when one attacked me from behind. I swiftly picked, amongst the many weapons, a club which I swung real hard smashing a head while the horse from nowhere trampled on the remaining two. My chest busted with courage as I helped Till fight with a club that gave me so much strength. Till was really impressed, and we conquered them. I felt so weak, but Till insisted we continue, our trails had just begun.

And so I wondered…what more was to come?

We kept moving, the forest became darker now, and we had not encountered anything new. We were moving slowing on a loop around the forest then leaves began to fall above our heads, wet leaves. I tasted one as it fell on my lip, it was so sweet, then, I started feeling dizzy and my lips felt so heavy. All I remember hearing while I almost fell off my horse was Till calling out to me until I felt his arms around me and he kept whispering these words " you will be fine."

I woke up in the dark perceiving smoke with so much of it stored in my lungs. I coughed profusely. Apparently, we were in a cave and Till was beside me arranging a pile of twigs to put in the fire.

"What happened?" I asked.

"Huh!...you tasted the leaf of a tree we call *kamal*. A tree the gods planted to give sleep, but, too much of it leads to eternal sleep. Lucky you, you had just a taste."

I smiled when I heard the word lucky since I felt so lucky but Till looked so weary, I just had to ask.

"Worried about your people?"

He sighed before he responded

"Of course I am, Uya. My quest for so much has hurt my loved ones and enemies alike. I need to redeem them."

When he mentioned 'loved ones' I remembered home, my mother and how she must be so worried about my whereabouts.

"Till, can we continue the mission please...I want to go home."

I sounded like a lost two-year old and he stared at me like a father with a child with no mother.

"Of course, Uya."

We stepped out of the cave with lamps in our hands. The horses were tied to some branches outside the cave. We mounted our horses and continued the journey steadily. While we journeyed across two rivers all stacked with carnivorous fishes, we were being drawn to a soothing melody. It sounded like a group of women humming in harmony plunging the ears and the soul and wrapping it in a melody. Till was drawn to it, so was I. and it seems our horses were too because they followed the music. We began to pass through a thick forest in search of the melody until we found ourselves dazed in the midst of the forest, lost in the melody and then suddenly, it stopped. There was absolute silence. Even the birds did not sing, but then in seconds, we saw ropes falling over our heads and then a large net landing over us. Suddenly, Till started screaming "it's the Habitsu…habitsu. oh why did I forget?" sounding so afraid and lost. "I have fully failed my people" he continued, sounding all hopeless.

"What's going on Till?" I asked in anxiety while I tried to get out of the net free, "what's wrong?" I insisted.

"The Habitsu are seductresses who hunt and kill for game. We are dead."

He said this with his eyes already overwhelmed with tears and sorrow and his heart filled with disappointment, I , on the contrary did not want to believe the verdict and so I kept trying to tear the net and all Till said was "there is no use". Before we knew it we began to see people approach us while others were sliding down the tall trees. I have never seen women who looked more beautiful. They were dressed in rags, covering their breasts and rear, all had long hair with either shiny blue or green eyes. Tall with elegance and their bodies were shaped to perfection but then, the beast did not seize to show itself when they came to lift us in the net. They had claws and pangs like a snake, they hissed at us while they wagged their long thick tongues. We were lifted with sticks hooked to the rope, I think they were seven who did. I have never seen Till look so sad and weak, and it was then I was certain that we had no hope.

The walk seemed to be long because we slept on the way, and by the time I woke up I saw a place, a place that had so much red that the sky looked like it. They had heads hung on stakes at the entrance; they seemed fresh as blood was still dripping down. The heads were arranged in array on a slope. It was so frightening as we walked past. I had never missed home that much. I began to think of my mother and how she made sure I was always happy, making me my favourite meals and clothing me with the best. I then thought of my friends and school, how I would miss them and all the activities and also, I thought of my father and how I would meet him soon. Tears began to roll and I wondered how I got swayed to this. Suddenly, we were dropped on the ground. It hurt so badly when we landed. We were halted in front of a hut. The ground was muddy; I wondered if blood was their moisture…then, she came out. She glowed like the sun. Poor Till was even blinded by it. Soft and beautiful, dressed in a silver rag covering her chest and the rear, she looked way better than the rest with eyes that glitters like gold. I smiled despite my predicament and I was even awed when she spoke. Such poise and elegance, a fine description of beauty, but in my mind I was certain that she was more deadly than a viper.

She spoke to her subordinates in a strange language and one of them, who seemed to be 'the general' of the 'army' answered her. She then turned to us.

"What's your name?" she asked softly, running her fingers through my hair with a sweet smile.

"My name…is…Uya," I stammered.

"What's your mission?"

I slowly raised my head in response in a bid to look confident.

"We are on a quest to break an ancient curse, please, please do not kill us."

"O, no, no... little girl, I won't kill you but I am thinking I may need your man for a sacrifice I need to perform. Therefore, am letting you go now."

I was distorted, wondering how a woman will let a child walk through this lonely, scary path alone but lest I forget, she has the instinct of a warrior.

"Please, sweet lady, don't kill Till."

I sounded so sober and then she snapped in surprise.

" Till..." she emphasized, "the notorious Till who cursed his land for love."

She walked towards him while she spoke smiling, bewildered making Till sound like a 'hero'.

"I have heard your stories...hmmm, let them go."

The ladies were surprised, murmuring and wondering why while they cut us loose.

"Now, go before I change my mind."

We wondered what she was doing but we ran. Till drag his feet but we ran and when we were far, I shouted "thank you!"

We walked in silence after that plight and a few miles into our tiring work as we crawled in hunger and thirst we saw a red light in a distance and a lions roar. Immediately we saw the light, I saw a smile of relief on Till's face and before he could speak, the lions roared and then he said "we are doomed". I asked why but he insisted I remained silent while we quietly walked towards the direction of the light. At that moment, the hunger and thirst was forgotten, our lives were more important. Safely, we reached the spot where the light reflected from and behold, it was my house and there was the staff not below but beside and at the spot Till always pointed at. Though spooky, my house was the only house in the midst of the forest with no one in. The staff had a red stone as its head, surrounded by dew at its feet and seven huge lions guarding it which were assumed to have been guarding my ancestor.

"That is what we came for... are you ready?" Till asked.

I was frightened suddenly and having cold feet, felt like I was lost at that moment he asked because I had never seen lions look so huge and angry.

"Ready for what Till?" I stuttered.

"I will create a distraction," he said, "then, you will go past these lions and prick the index finger of your left hand on the red glittering stone...then, all will be free. Here's the knife. Go!"

I left, hesitantly.

Stealthily, I walked away, awaiting his distraction. Suddenly, I heard a loud thud and he was in the midst of these lions. They roared so loud and then he lifted his sword in defence as they pounced on him. Quickly, I walked towards the staff although sceptical as its surrounding was so serene. I pricked my index finger, however painful, I have forgotten but as soon as my blood dropped on the red stone there was a loud beagle and then, the lions vanished. Then, a swift wind blew me off my feet and I was twirling round and round as though I was in a tornado, illuminating me. Then, I heard a loud thank you of a thousand people as I moved in the wind. I closed my eyes.

"Uya! Uya!!...wake up! You have school to go to," said my mother while I woke up touching my body to ensure it was real.

"Mama, How long have I been asleep?" I asked anxiously with the need to be told I was in a coma.

"What do you mean?" she said. "It's morning and you need to go to school."

I wondered if this was all a dream, it felt so real.

"Mmm...Uya, who is the man with the white hat? You kept saying his name in your sleep," she said while she organized my kit for school.

Silly me, I thought, it was all a dream.

Bond Free

I

THE CONFERENCE ROOM
THE GOLDEN ROOM

If anyone had said to me, that I and Bode will be where we are today, I would have laughed. Who remembers the days we had ice cream on the rocks? Such excitement, so much laughter. Or, the days we had to chase those sheep and put our posters on them - "vote for Pius and Bode! For president and vice president of the SUG"...so many tales, so many smiles yet, life had its package for us.

How many of you understand the word greed? Blind sadness or better yet, envy, intense bitterness. My heart aches when I realize that these and more took away that guy that I respected and trusted! The one I called a best friend.

The great UNIBEN; the university of Benin was where we first met. A shy tiny boy, not too fresh out of secondary school, I had been at home for close to three years before I got admitted into the university to study Chemistry. The auditorium was a hall of so many reminders, talking about it makes me laugh within and yes, it was the first place I met Bode. He was certainly not as tiny but yet I admired his courage and agility to get things done in a hurry. I noticed

28

him walk out of the auditorium swiftly that day when I walked up to him believing he knew what he was doing.

"Bros, what's up?!" I said being a bit cautious.

"Hey! Am good" he said giving me a handshake simultaneously. I explained on how lost I was in the process and although he was in the social sciences to study political science he was my guide every step of the way, and that's how we began. We were brothers from different mothers, felt like a definition of Siamese twins. Even women could not come in between. We had no girlfriends and we didn't make them a focus rather we kept acquaintances and a very few close.

In three hundred level, when I was contesting for the position of president of my department, he was there every step of the way. Placing my fliers in different corners of the school. We sneaked at night to do it together, he was so excited even more than I was. I guess he saw this as a forum to be practical on his field of study especially when it came to the campaign. It was so dramatic, with the general populace assuming that he was the actual contestant but seeing the posters they realized he wasn't. I liked the idea that he was a part of my team and it made me more confident, and I owed my victory to him. Then came final year, the hunger for more made me contest for the president of the Student Union Congress. He supported the idea. We shared like minds in ambition and I heartily made him my vice. When the time came, we organized rallies bringing all our friends and neighbours for support. We had our fliers everywhere and even made friends with lectures we never thought we would. The process was quite hectic and expensive. Our entire savings was dived into it with us going hungry on countless occasions but, who would know?

I had an opponent, Davis Rume. He was a student of History and I must confess being an opponent I was hopeless on his case. He was extremely popular, indulging himself in every activity both intellectual and social. Who didn't love him? Most of all, he was tall and handsome with eloquence, certainly every girl's dream in comparison to myself a tiny looking guy with no zest for such. Its like when I put efforts into doing all that Davis does , just to appeal to the public, I muddled things more and so, I stopped! But, Bode was wonderful at that time, he gave me the boost of a giant when I felt so little and intimidated.

"Guy! No tell me say that Davis dey intimidate you?" he asked one day while we sat to draw an agenda.

"No be say I dey fear am guy...it's just that, it's just that I need..." I stuttered while I averted my face to save myself from seeing the disappointment in his.

"O boy...no shame me! No shame me at all! Na that dumb boy you wan give room to?!" He sounded so disappointed and provoked. I felt emasculated but it was a challenge and I had a plan. I had to be more confident but little did I know that Bode had his.

I was seated one day doing my laundry when I heard a ping from my blackberry, it was a video. The video was from a contact of mine and then beneath it he said," You don win!". I was confused. Given the election was three weeks ahead and I had a strong opponent, I wondered what he meant. Opening the video, my heart jumped! It was a video of Davis smoking weed and sniffing some with material on a girl's arms which I suspect to be cocaine and the I wondered, who took this video? When and how?

As exhilarated as I felt, I was sincerely uncomfortable and worried. I was so certain that this will draw a storm, a storm I was not ready to control. The video went viral alright, a wide broadcast even as far as other institutions. I could not wait to tel Bode. After I had concluded my laundry and had a shower, I dashed down to his apartment. I found him acting more joyous than usual. Dancing incoherently to song on the back ground with a couple of our friends, and I knew that moment what his excitement was and all I did was join in.

"O boy! See how victory fall for our lap *gbam*!" He said while he rested his arms on my shoulders and I laughed.

That night when I returned home, I found Davis at my door step seated, looking all sober and distraught. The thought of laughing at him or asking questions on why he had to be so stupid and careless was not my burden rather, I pitied him. The handsome fellow looked so wrinkled and beaten like a chicken under the rain.

"Davis," I cleared my throat, "what is wrong?"

I sounded empathetic. Before now, myself and Davis did not see eye to eye. The tension that was between us made the struggle for the position seem bloody but here he was today at my door step, seated by my draft board.

"They said politics is a dirty game," he said while he played with the seeds on the draft board, "and it truly is" he sighed. "I do not remember what I see in the video Pius and I will prefer it if you quit pretending that you do not know what's going down. I back out from this race, but, for the sake of posterity…" He rose from his seat and walked towards me, resting his hand on my right shoulder "beware". And then he walked away. I stood in silence wondering if he just threatened me or gave me a future warning. That word always rang in my head, even till this moment that I am a father.

The election took place alright, and it was a flawless victory for us. Interestingly, I never told Bode about my encounter with Davis, I thought I'll be a sissy doing that or better yet a "snitch".

We had a successful tenure of one year. Although I would not deny the fact that we encountered so many financial dramas including accusations of swindling from the school's treasury . Being best friends the populace assumed that we had a financial flow among ourselves and we did not want to share. So much drama when it comes to money, but, we did all we could and fulfilled the small promises we made and I must confess, we satisfied a majority.

Out of sight was not out of mind for myself and Bode even when we were posted to different states to serve our Father land. He was posted to Kaduna and I was posted to Rivers state. Thank God for the social media, pinging made us better.

While I served in the city of Port Harcourt, I came across a beautiful lady, Tanya by name. Can't forget her, not even when I try. Fair skinned, with long legs that can embrace a nation. She had the countenance of a pagan goddess and a smile that swept me off my feet. I met her in a supermarket while I shopped for the weekend. She was so friendly, my heart skipped a bit every minute she spoke, making me shiver by the sound of her voice, it certainly was not obvious though but I think the joy in my eyes was.

We saw each other on a daily basis. I wondered why a woman that beautiful will still be single and I was certain that men were just too blind for my liking. She was so intelligent and also scrupulous especially in her analysis and her perception of things specifically politics which intrigued me. I had to tell Bode about her, and so, I took pictures of her and sent to him. I wonder what he was feeling but I got an unusual response from him. He called a day after I sent the picture without replying any of my messages.

"Where you see this babe Pius?"

He sounded gruffly but I summed it as he probably having a bad day.

"Na one babe for PH-o! We are somewhat neighbours."

"Okay. Enjoy."

And then, he hung up, abruptly. I was quite marvelled with no questions on what the drama meant.

Three days later, he called me, saying he was visiting Port Harcourt the next day and I should be ready to host him. I was extremely glad.

When he arrived Port Harcourt, I prepared a grand reception for him. Not what you have in mind but rather I bought plenty food and drinks with my small allowance just to ensure he enjoyed his stay. He told me his stay will be brief and that besides visiting he wanted to run away from Kaduna, especially the village where he was posted to Kwoi. I laughed at his stories. We stayed all night talking about our individual camp experiences and yes, the ladies. We barely slept that night, reminiscing while we sipped on alcohol and chewed some crackers. We were quite jolly.

Well, the next day I had to give him a tour. I had studied the town well enough to give him one. From Ikwere Road, where I stayed to Olu Obasanjo, Rumuola, Rumouokoro and Choba. It was an exhausting ride. By time we returned home it was late in the evening and while we entered the compound Bode began to ask questions about Tanya.

"Ehen, guy...where is that girl now? Your Tanya girl"

"Ah! She dey. I was hoping I visit her today but, its already late."

" Are you for real?!" He said, with that same tone when we were on Davis' case.

"Yes now! This is past ten and its highly ungentlemanly to intrude on a lady by this time."

"Where is her house then?!" He asked. I pointed towards the left, with her apartment quite close to mine except that she had a gate and I didn't.

Early in the morning, I had to prepare for work. My primary assignment then was being a chemistry teacher and given I had taken permission the previous day to be away from the school, I had to be there. So, I left Bode alone at home and the power that day was stable, he had no reason to be bored. Although I offered I take him to the school I taught but then he turned me down swiftly. While I dressed up, I heard a knock on my door and it was Tanya. She looked as beautiful as always making my heart skip. I only wished I had the courage to ask her on a date, but, I think my liver was absent. When Bode saw her, he couldn't take his eyes off her either, he almost stuttered when she had hello. That morning she said she came around to talk with me, saying how bored she was sitting at home. According to her, that was sometime before this moment, she had to resign from her job as a secretary because her boss was making passes at her and it went as far as threats.

I felt bad that I wasn't going to be around and so, I introduced her to Bode.

"I'll go to my apartment now." She said "But, you are welcome if you choose to visit". We all smiled at the offer, meanwhile I was extremely late and so I dashed out of the house to work.

The children were something else, anytime I think of them I smile. They were all " Uncle! Uncle!! Uncle!!!". After three hours in school I then remembered I gave the children an assignment and while I pondered on the solution they submitted their works. My head was too tensed to decipher solutions, so, I decided to return home in a hurry. When I returned home, Bode was not in the room. He had the place all cleaned up but then, I was certain he was with Tanya and so I decided to check on them briefly.

Tanya's gate was half way open. As I walked in, all I heard was faint screams and I thought it was a movie, and while I moved closer hearing the scream become louder I knew it wasn't a movie, it was Tanya in pangs. I ran towards her door which was open as well and while I found my way to her room, the screaming stopped. I tip toed to her bedroom from where I heard the sound, and forcing the door open I saw a dead girl with a smashed head. Lying half-naked with her clothes shredded, with blood spilled all over staining the white wall and there was Bode, standing above her body wielding a hammer.

"I told her I travelled all the way from Kaduna to see her, but she didn't believe me" he said angrily while he stared at her body. I was too speechless to talk. My mouth was agog with blank thoughts, no words. I looked at him, I felt he had gone mad "what the hell did you do man?!" I asked while tears rolled down my cheeks.

"I just wanted a taste."

He sounded like a psychopath; I could not believe my ears.

"Let's get out of here, now!"

We dashed out in a hurry with Bode still holding the hammer in his hands. We ran into my room consciously checking out for witnesses. I pushed him straight into the shower and by time he finished, we had to think fast.

"Guy, you need to turn yourself over to the police," I said.

" Are you mad!!! You dey mad?! Or you want me to scatter your brains too? Don't you dare forget all that I have done for you. We will handle this mess together."

"Together?! Are you listening to yourself? Isn't because I have not yet punched your teeth's out or better yet collect the hammer wey dey your hand and smash your brains?! You just killed a woman, a beautiful woman for no reason. And you are saying "together". Na u dey mad!"

Bode had never seen me that angry before, he knew he had to sort his thoughts.

"Pius, calm down. Abeg. Now, wetin we go do?" I looked at him, he sounded and acted sober. Suddenly, thoughts started rolling in; if we leave the body lying there and the police come around I'll be their first suspect because the people on the street know how friendly we are. And if we bury her body and get the place all cleaned up, no one will know, in fact, I will say she travelled.

"Guy! Our only solution na to bury her body in her back yard and then, we clean the walls and everywhere for any trace of blood."

Bode jumped at the idea and so we went to her apartment immediately to get things done. What marvelled me more was Bode's unremorseful attitude; it looked like he took pleasure in doing what he did and was satisfied making me a part of it. I then remembered those days back in school when I virtually had to beg him to stop giving women black eyes. I had girls come to complain to me when he was the vice president of the Student Union Government of how he had raped them and pleaded with them not to tell anyone but gave them money as consolation, but, they could not hide their pains anymore. I spoke to him about this and then he promised that he would change and I did see a bit of that as there were no more complains for a while ,he acted like he was in control of that part of him, little did I know that he was breeding a bigger demon.

We buried Tanya's body behind her house. The little I could do was to clean her body of the blood and quickly wear her a dress, and as I did so, I began to nurse hatred for Bode. It was building up like a candle light illuminating a dark room. As he spoke comfortably while we cleaned his mess, I said nothing. I worked in silence. By time we finished, it was already evening and while we tried to dust ourselves we heard a knock on the gate. I suspected that it was her boyfriend, because he kept saying "Baby! Bae!!" We locked the gate and so he couldn't enter. We also switched off her phone. When we were certain that he had left, we ran out, locking every door. As for the gate, we closed it carelessly. When we entered the apartment, Bode began to laugh loudly. I thought he was truly insane.

"Did you see that?" he said while he continued to laugh. "I wondered what would have happened if he had seen us and known what's up. He for form superman," pushing out his chest in demonstration.

I had no words for him, I only nodded my head. I was so hungry, but I couldn't eat. I kept seeing Tanya's face and there tears began to roll. What have I done? Bode kept ranting and talking to himself, I don't remember all he said but then, I decided to speak.

"You are going back to Kaduna Bode, tomorrow morning!"

"But, Guy?!"

"I mean it Bode!" I yelled. " You need to leave."

In the morning, I packed his things for him, not listening to anything he had to say. I stopped an *okada* in front of my house and then I told the bike man to take him to Rumukoro park and from there he could find his way to the general park.

"Good bye Bode." I said " Our friendship is over!" He was too shocked to reply me but, I didn't look backwards. Quickly, I ran into my house, packed all my belongings and in thirty minutes I gave out those I could not carry. I quickly called a cab man with whom I was friendly with and I moved to stay in a motel a distance away from my former apartment which was reserved for corpers.

I don't know if Tanya's body was ever found, but I know that since that day till this moment, I see her in my dreams, my thoughts and even in my late wife. My conscience eats me on a daily but I couldn't share this story. As for Bode, we never spoke again, he called countlessly but I did not return any of his calls, until this moment where you all say you do not consider me fit to be governor of Edo state because you have a criminal charge and a witness which is my dear friend, Bode. So, from my testimony, what is your conclusion?

II

CONFERENCE ROOM

THE SILVER ROOM

The air was tensed with all the men of council who were five in number, wearing wrinkled faces staring sternly at Bode. He was on a wheel chair, wearing worn out clothes and his hair looking rough like he was practicing on dread locks.

" He killed that girl!" Said Bode, obviously standing firm at his accusation.

"Mr .Bode!" said an elderly council member, responding impatiently," Your accusation does not count! You have repeatedly said 'he killed that girl' with no meaningful head way. And from what I see, you look like you have lost your mind. What's your motive Mr. Bode?"

Bode sat in silence while he stared into his palms waiting for the words to come.

"Men of council...when I agreed to speak against a man who used to be my best friend, aligning with his opposition, Mr Osaze, I knew what I was doing. I know that as we speak, he is also being made to tell his side of the story, well, listen to mine. We were good friends alright, meeting at the auditorium we became friends instantly. Through the years in the political struggle, I spoke for him at most times, I was his protocol officer, his friend and everything to make a man feel safe. Although, I observed a feature in him, a feature I could not comprehend. It seemed like he was bipolar or just evil! He laughed at wickedness, never used the word 'sorry' and did not show mercy. If he did, it was for show, it was for ambition. Our three hundred level elections, when he went for the position of a departmental president was peaceful and less dramatic than the chase for the presidency of the Student Union Government. I saw his fears, his doubts and so, I did the right thing a true friend should. I met Davis on a certain day and asked we hangout in his house. I pretended I had grave issues with Pius and even said I was going to withdraw from Pius' team and join his. Davis was really carried away plus excited, and, rumour had it that he was a junkie at night and so I used that moment to test the rumours. Viola! He smoked and sniffed on all that I provided and then, I recorded every minute of it. Instantly, I made the video viral. I doubt if Pius is aware of this story. I did what I had to for the sake of ambition, for the sake of victory and yes, friendship. But what can I say, nothing lasts forever aye! "

The men in the Conference Room had their ears to the ground, waiting for Bode to say the words they wanted to hear badly. Bode continued speaking, expressing his emotions as the words came.

"I did visit Pius in Port Harcourt and we had a blast. I met Tanya too. She was very beautiful and I understood Pius' obsession for her. What I did not understand was his jealousy. He told me of how he was going to kill her boyfriend if he did not stop coming to see her. That he couldn't bear the thought of him touching her. And so, still a few days into my visit, I was watching a movie when he suddenly dashed into the room, in the evening, with blood all over his body and, he had a hammer in his hand covered in blood. And then I asked him what was going on? And all he said was "Guy! We need to clean a mess fast!!!" He was so frightened and fidgeted every step of the way and then, we buried her in her backyard. I did not kill her...please, I was only an accomplice. And all I see is her face everywhere I go and my conscience could not bear the guilt. I called Pius on several occasions after that day about seeing this girl and being unable to take her thoughts out of my head. You know what he did? He stopped picking my calls, the ingrate stopped picking my calls!!! I got mad, I then sent him text messages two years later when I learnt he was married and he already had a son, I said that I will go to the police and confess if he does not man up to do so. Three days later, I had a ghastly motor accident that made me loose my legs. Now, its three years since my accident and my dear Pius is a gubernatorial candidate; he does not deserve that, he doesn't! And that is why I am here to make you reconsider. Pius is not a man ...he is a monster!

The members of the council stared as he spoke, speechless. They watched him scratch his hair and legs and the wobble his lips. The head of the council suddenly looked at him in disgust.

"Mr Bode, I do not know why Mr Osaze thought that bringing you here will resolve certain issues or it's just his plain act of desperation! The council will not tolerate any form of childishness and stupidity. Whatever issues you have to resolve between yourselves, settle them! Pius still remains our candidate. As for you Osaze," he points his finger at him, "we have tolerated unbearable embarrassments from you, you will not spread this story. Pius has proven himself worthy, I wonder what you are waiting for."

All the other men of council nodded their heads in agreement, humming "hmmm". Bode wanted to speak, but the words did not come out. "Take this man out of our presence!" yelled the head of the council.

III

THE CONFERENCE GATE

Bode waited at he gate with his hands folded, wearing a face of disappointment. He clenched his fists like he was in deep regret with his eyes down to his feet. As he got lost in his thoughts he was suddenly startled by a hand resting on his shoulders.

"How interesting can life be?!" Pius said while he chuckled, using his left hand to adjust his tie. "Friendship is dead! There is no loyalty anymore."

"Don't you dare tell me about loyalty!" retorted Bode." What more destruction do you want to cause? After taking my legs and my life? You killed my wife man?!! Why?" He cried, "Did it have to go that far because I had to speak of Tanya or is it because I did not get to tell them what led to your wife's death as well?"

"You do not speak about my wife Bode!" He said angrily, grabbing him by the neck. He then withdraws his hand when he notices someone come towards the gate.

"Pius...I pity your soul. You will never get away with this!" Bode replied calmly.

"But I have Bode, I already have. I did not kill your wife my friend, your mouth did. I admit, Tanya's death was a delicious experience" he grinned, "An experience that must remain a story between the both of us. You know why? No one is sick enough to listen to your version! And, you see those pathetic old council men, eh...are all under my pay-cheque. Have a nice life Bode! And I wish you and Osaze a safe ride...cheers!"

He takes his sunglasses out of his breast pocket and wearing it, he walks away. Bode had his eyes full of hatred fixed on him as he walked away, looking powerless and in pain, he only teared at the end of the day.

Somewhere...Here

Tears roll down her eyes everyday she gets to stare at her only reason for existence, her only smile, a five year blessing, her daughter Oreli defiled by the cruel world.

She had no choice, she had to recover money from her sales. Her debtors were reluctant to pay their debts until this very day. The fruit business is quite competitive and tasking in Plateau state with every slice or bunch that comes with a price however little but important.

Grace was nineteen when she had Oreli. She got involved with the boy next door and *bam*! He denied he was the father. Her parents treated her with disdain calling her a disgrace, an ingrate and opting for abortion which she rejects. With no money or hope, she was kicked out of her family house. The streets were no comfort and then she thought of her grand-aunt, Miriam who heartily welcomed her into her home. The kind frail old lady was always receptive to relatives despite their rejection towards her because she never married nor bore a child. They nick-named her 'Zombie' a walking dead, but she never treated with hatred; call that being a saint. And so when Grace arrived and explained her situation Miriam was more than willing to accommodate her.

Time passed and eventually Grace gave birth with Miriam beside her every step of the way, through the delivery and growth of the little Oreli. When Oreli was two years old Miriam died of a heart attack leaving her possessions and properties in Grace's care.

Grace had frustration beaming in her eyes when she found her five year old daughter lying half dead by her fruit table. She had not been away for close to an hour only to return to a helpless child. The fruits enticingly displayed were untouched; the table was the same when she left. Her heart was overwhelmed with pain staring at her five year-old child lying with blood stains around her legs. She embraced her child in tears shivering and praying that what she thought this was is not so. "*Ore... Ore, mai ya faru*? Hmmm... my baby" she whispered softly .

Grace barely concluded her secondary school education, graduating with two credits in Food and Nutrition and Agriculture. The rest were a float of failures. She had a better knowledge of the Hausa language with good understanding for Pidgin English and less knowledge for English which she had no interest in. Her mother always emphasized on the benefits of education which she seemed to have taken for granted.

Oreli stared into her mother's eyes with tears and catarrh rolling down simultaneously, pitifully. She sniffed in every catarrh that dripped quivering as she spoke.

"Mama" she said, "Uncle Monday, da Uncle Romo da Uncle Steven da... da Uncle Davou da Uncle Tawe, *sun... sun hawo mun jiki sai suna ta cuka wani abu Kaman sanda a cikin duri na. Mama, Mama yana mun zafi...*" she stammered and cried as she remembered the scenario, with no energy left to express her agony.

Grace lifted her to her thighs and laid her head on her chest, rowing back and forth while they cried together. How could the world be so cruel? Five middle aged men robbing a child of its innocence. Grace knew she had to do something and the police came to mind. The police station was a stone throw away and conveniently Grace backed her daughter and headed for the station.

The station was empty, all doors were open but no soul seemed to have been around. The building is quite small with numerous exits and a small room they call a cell. Grace opted for remaining at the reception believing someone will surface and in no time, her faith worked for her. She heard them trooping in from another wing of the station. Grace swiftly rose to her feet when she realized they were truly the police, two policemen precisely. In excitement she narrated her situation to the police hoping at the back of her mind that justice was hers.

"What's your proof of rape Madame?" one of the policemen asked looking disgusted at her inability to express herself. Grace on the other hand was flabbergasted wondering if they were so blind not to see her child in her helpless state.

"Oga police, see my pickin...eh? See how them tear her clothes, see blood Oga...see blood," she reiterated, tearing as she wiped her face with her wrapper.

The second policeman chuckled at her expression "Madame". He said obviously impatient, "We have a lot of work to do, you sure sey no be you do all these things for your pickin body to incriminate them...eh?

Grace's mouth was opened in surprise to their response. What happened to the police is your friend? None with the courtesy to even console her or assure her? She adjusted Oreli on her back and without hesitation but in humiliation walked out of the police station in silence leaving the police men hissing and throwing jabs at her.

Grace stood in the middle of the road, wondering where to go from thence. Suddenly, she sighted a hospital from afar and it clicked! She quickly stopped a passing bike and headed straight for the hospital. Oreli rested calmly on her mother's back, sleep has a way of making one forget one's worries. Grace was glad at her child's disposition and the serenity that enveloped her, sleep may have helped her forget but Grace feared what followed.

The reception at the hospital has warm. The matron they encountered acted so motherly enquiring if the case was reported to the police but was disappointed at the response. "how could people be so cruel and impetuous!" she said with Grace wondering what 'impetuous' was. The matron quickly informed the only female pediatrician in the hospital about the child. Her name was doctor Tola, quite compassionate in her relationship with her patients. She was filled with concern and pity when she heard of Oreli. Swiftly, she ordered for a stretcher on which Oreli was lifted and taken to the emergency unit.

"Madame" she said "your daughter will be fine. It's a good thing you came by. I'll check her as soon as possible but you have to make some small payments."

Grace stared at Doctor Tola awed at her beauty but weary that her funds would not be enough to procure the bills.

"okay Doctor... I get 5000 naira, na de money I suppose use buy fruits, e go do?"

"Yes..." she replied calmly "meet with the receptionist. I need to go run some tests on your daughter."

Grace was thankful she had the money tied in a fold in her wrapper because with private hospitals, no excuse works.

Grace sat at the reception, comforted that her child was in care but worried that her daughter may not be the same again. O how her heart soiled with hate for every man especially those men. The urge to avenge her child ran through her veins but she had no courage to accomplish that.

The wait at the reception was getting tiring with no sign of anyone to tell her about Oreli's condition. She was elated when she saw Doctor Tola come out of the EU. The doctor walked up to her and said "Madame, could you follow me to my office please?"

She looked quite serious when making the request.

Grace's heart skipped a beat, she had seen such scenarios on television and it usually did not turn so well. The doctor's office was quite tidy with paraphernalia of toys on her shelf and a candy jar on her desk. Grace was marveled by it all that she stared around admiring how colorful the office was.

"Please sit Madame," Doctor Tola said, wearing an indifferent look. "Your daughter is in severe pains but she will be fine. But she will be under our watch for a few days. We intend to have a series of tests on her."

Grace listened, but turned worried when the doctor told her of her bill. She refused to burden her thoughts as she asked to see Oreli instead.

"She is asleep," Doctor Tola said while clearing out her desk and then she paused staring at the distressed woman when she said "Madame, God will see you through and give you justice. Be easy." The words seemed to have consoled

Grace and she held on to them as she headed for the public children's ward where Oreli was moved to. Her heart was filled with joy staring at her daughter sleep so peacefully wearing a smile. Grace wondered if someone was making her truly happy in her dreams, she wished for the smile to linger.

Grace sat by Oreli, holding her daughter's hand to her face, kissed it and said: "God go give you justice my pikin, God go give you justice."

The Lone Miner

Her head was down to the ground as she gazed into the soil. She was lost in her thoughts and every movement in the mines sounded like echoes. Then a cockroach came out of nowhere dragging its hind and finding it difficult to walk. *Allow me save you the trouble my friend; it's a cold, cold world.* She crushes it. Covering it with sand and continued her gaze.

"Kaneng! Kaneng!!" yelled a male voice as he walked towards her ardently. "Kaneng what are you doing here?! The tin is littered all over and it's your responsibility to clean it up! Get your pan and get to work!!"

She stared at Mr Wilson with her round, brown, bulgy eyes as he demonstrated angrily, pointing his hands in different directions trying to control over a hundred workers who were obviously exhausted and worn out. There was no water to drink. The woman who sold *kunu* did not come around early. She was tired; tired of her work, tired of her life, tired of being silent. At twenty five, she already wished she had three children if not five, with a hearty husband and a large farm land but how could she get that when she had only one arm. Who would marry a handicap? People often called her beautiful, saying her dark long thick kinky hair was that of a queen and so was her slender frame and face, but she found it truly hard to believe. The tin mine was all she had and all she knew. She was trained to believe in the essence of tin and its usefulness to the earth, and so, she held on to her knowledge of it. Her father, DA Davou, says to her countlessly, "Enjoy the gift of nature which is the priceless gift on the plateau. Men have no value for it...cherish it." Her father was so sentimental about it and she wondered why.

The texture of tin marvelled her mind though, and how it glittered when in water, sparkling as it flows, thus, it worried her to see men who had no value for it waste some away but, what could she say or do? She had no money, she had no voice.

Kaneng spent most of her time alone, drawing in the sand whenever she is in the mine. She watched people hold hands and her female colleagues gossip hopelessly, sadly she had no words, she had no place and they looked like they were perfect in the right number and so, she did not participate.

Her eyes viewed the world as a place of pain, filled with so much unfairness and ruin cause if it were not so, why was life so unfair to take her arm after that ghastly motor accident. All she did was to cross the road on her way to her father's farm, she was so happy then, jumping back and forth with her hoe resting on her shoulders on the main road that leads to other villages in plateau and beyond. She was only sixteen, basking in the warmth of the early sun and watching her growing breasts joggle in excitement. As she danced on the empty road all alone and trying to pick her hoe which fell on the ground, a rover came in speed and swept her off her feet. She felt the world had cheated her; the driver did not have the courtesy of picking her and taking her to the nearest clinic. Blurringly, she watched him stop abruptly as she laid helplessly on the road with blood spouting out of her mouth.

He came down, felt her pulse and when he was certain she had life in her, he looked around to see if anyone was watching and then, he ran to his vehicle and drove off. Tears rolled down her eyes silently, she wondered if this was how she was going to die. As she sealed her eyes in pain, she opened it in time to realize that she was in the hospital and her father was beside her. She smiled when she saw him and truly thankful to him. She knew that this was a known responsibility for a mother, but where was hers? Where was she when she needed her so dearly and why did she leave her father? Her Father said her reason was because she was not happy but what about her?

Kaneng's mother, Chundung, was a known retailer for jewels and stones. She came from an ancestry of royalty and she did not appreciate her husband, DA Davou, even into their marriage with the excuse that he had nothing more to offer her. He loved her hopelessly but with every moment she stared into his eyes, all she saw was how poor he had become.

"You irritate me Davou! I can't believe that I married you thinking that we would make some money someday. Look at your mates!!! Will I keep feeding you?"

Those were the words Kaneng woke up to everyday since she was five until her mother left when she was ten. The words came out with so much hate and disgust and it made the tears flow bitterly for Kaneng and worst in the soul of Davou. Chundung had to leave, she packed her things one morning and left without a "goodbye", she just left.

Kaneng's world was like a circle of ice in a dirty bottle, she felt that way. Cold and rejected, forgotten by a world she had so much hope for, she had no reason to see the light. Any man who takes a glimpse at her seems to irritate her, all she felt was mockery and pang. The few friends she had she barely said hello to, and they were basically her neighbours.

"Kaneng! Welcome-o!" said Rosemary, a neighbour of hers who made it a responsibility to check her and greet her heartily. As pleasant as Rosemary sounded, Kaneng was not drawn to her, neither was she carried away by the smiles she shared. All she wanted to do everyday after work was to sit beside the charcoal fire with her father and watch it burn. The flames felt like a consolation, a reminder that there will be light! The warmth made her feel safe, free from any thought that will fill her soul with bitterness and then, sleep, sleep embraces her and she forgets that she ever existed.

Everyday in the mines was an adventure, with Mr Wilson regularly being a busy body. It made Kaneng smile most times when he yells and raises his jumpy trousers simultaneously. Mr Wilson was a stout man, naturally aggressive and insecure. It worried Kaneng every time when he always asks irrelevant questions just to ensure that he was secure. He seemed to care less about the workers, all he wanted was for the tin moved and sieved so that his bosses, who were Lebanese, will return and see what he has done and probably take him along to Lebanon or wherever they may live. He did not see water as a priority neither was food, he felt whatever he paid was enough to provide all of that for them.

"Oga!" said Manji, the fellow leading the miners, "water no dey...and we wan drink water."

Wilson stands with his arms akimbo looking ahead and pretending to ignore this tall fellow who seems to intimidate him with his height.

"Don't I pay you enough?! Don't I pay you enough

everyday?!" he retorted.

"But Sir..."

"Don't Sir Me! Wait for your next round of payment and then, you can buy whatever you want, in the mean time...work!"

The mines reminded Kaneng of the stories she had heard about the slave trade, it's just sad that it is no longer the white men who do so but her fellow black man. All for the greed of more, more money and power to subdue. She is usually more disgusted when the Lebanese arrive and Mr Wilson gravels to greet them and so did every other worker, and she watches them throw fifty and hundred naira notes on their faces, yet, they are exceedingly grateful. She knew her pride will not stoop low, even as she is one-armed.

Mr Kashmir, one of the Lebanese men who came to the mines frequently, took time to observe Kaneng. He wondered why she was silent most times and it intrigued him. He tries flashing a smile once in awhile but Kaneng pays no attention, seems she considered it an insult, until one day.

"Hello," he said, trying to sound friendly and staring at Kaneng while she waited for her turn to receive tin for sieving. "How are you?"

Kaneng looked uncomfortable and wondered what was his problem.

"I am fine," she replied, finding it difficult to look back into his eyes.

"Can you leave what you are doing so we could talk?"

"Okay," she gulped. Her colleagues on the queue had their eyes on them as they walked away with a few chorusing hmmmm...

Mr Kashmir walked slowly with her out of the mines

under the mild weather, as he asked her a few questions which got her troubled.

"You are a beautiful woman," he said firmly.

Kaneng was too stunned to reply, despite feeling uncomfortable and shy, she felt he was making a fool of her.

"Why are you so quiet? I noticed you do not associate with any of your colleagues, may I know why?"

Kaneng began to clench her fist, feeling nervous. She remembered when she heard some of her colleagues say how Mr. Kashmir could not seal his eyes to anyone who wears a skirt. He seemed to fall for anyone or anything, the rumours were he had been involved with a few women in the mines and he did not apologize for the drama.

"Sir, you dey ask me plenty questions o...I don't know why?"

Mr. Kashmir laughed loudly. It sounded like he had not laughed in awhile. As they walked towards a bamboo tree which had a bench beneath it he offered they sit. Kaneng stood beside the bench refusing to sit while she fidgets.

"Please sit down," Mr Kashmir said politely.

Kaneng still stood beside the bench with her arms folded paying a deaf ear to his request.

"Sit down my friend!" he yelled, making Kaneng shake in fear as she slowly sat on the bench. "Better... You Africans enjoy being yelled at, I don't know why."

He moved closer to her.

"I find you very intriguing Kaneng, and I want us to be friends."

Kaneng jumped off her seat in fear and discomfort, looking around just in case the trees had ears.

" Oga Kashmir...I am begging you, please, please leave

me. I don't want any friend," she said quietly, sounding pitiful.

Mr. Kashmir looked at her like she was overtly dramatic and wearing a wry smile he just watched her look so nervous and moving her feet like she was about to race away.

"Kaneng," he sighed, "I acknowledge how naive you may be and all the rumours you must have heard about me, which I have heard of as well and I am truly shocked about, but I don't see you in that way. My words will not be enough, let's just see how things go."

"Hmmm...Oga Kashmir, grammar," she grumbled.

When Kaneng returned home that night sitting by the fire side with her father, she began to think of Mr. Kashmir. "What did he want?" What did he mean as a friend?" Suddenly, the place that used to feel warm and safe was beginning to suffocate her. She did not know when she left abruptly leaving her father in sudden worry.

By time it was morning, she thought the previous days affair was a dream. It felt like she was in a different world, and her usual gloom countenance changed to an aggressive one. She walked out of the house without saying good bye to her father who awaits her to do so before going to work. She stormed out wearing a furious face until she got to the mines. Her heart skipped a beat when she sighted Mr. Kashmir walking towards her with a couple of her colleagues by his side, attending to his needs. It was unusual for him to be around this early in the morning, she knew she could not take the insults any more, she just had to voice it out.

"Oga," she said as he walked towards her, almost a feet away, "Oga, can I see you?"

"Excuse me?!" He replied gruffly, acting like he had not

known her. "Young lady, it is either you get back to work or face my wrath, talk to me indeed!"

And he walked pass her like she was invisible.

Kaneng marvelled at the new situation, felt like she was dreaming again, too good to be true. The frown she wore suddenly turned to a baffled face. Severally as Mr Kashmir passed, she will steal a glimpse at him to observe if he had seen her or he was pretending and Mr. Kashmir on the other hand seemed not to care at all. She then decided not to bother anymore. While she waited on the queue for her turn to fetch tin for sieving, she was suddenly alerted.

"Kaneng!" said one of her male colleagues tapping her on her shoulders, "*Oga* Kashmir dey call you?!"

Her eyes widened in dismay and then she felt something was wrong with the man after all.

She walked to his office which was immediately cleared of people when she walked in.

"Sit down," Mr. Kashmir said politely, motioning that she sat opposite him. His eyes rolled at her body, seizing her from head to toe, and she sat uncomfortably with her head bowed down.

"Am sorry I pretended not to know you. It's our work place so, let work be work and pleasure, pleasure," he said, while he smiled enjoying her silence. Suddenly, he rose from his seat and locked the door behind them; it seemed he signalled for everyone to leave the premises because of the overwhelming silence that surrounded them. Mr Kashmir's office was made of red bricks with paraphernalia of wooden items which include his furniture and the shelf beside his office table. The office smelled like roses with a blend of dry leaves which made the office feel cold. Kaneng wanted to jump out of her seat the moment she heard the door lock and when she felt him come behind her slowly; she was certain that her life was over, she never knew how.

"Kaneng...Kaneng! Am I right?" he asked, while he rested his hands on her shoulders, massaging them while she shrugged. "You are playing hard to get?! I like that!"

He walks away from her back and then sits on the table, facing her.

"You know, the first time I saw you, I realized that having two arms does not necessarily make you complete, you are a hero with one arm and you still do what people with both arms do, and I admire you for that."

Kaneng sat mute still, finding it hard to look at Mr. Kashmir who was directly facing her and they were barely two inches apart. Her heart beat faster than the engines of a machine, it felt like it was about to pull out of its place.

" I like you Kaneng, I hope you know," as he caressed her cheek.

"Oga Kashmir...What...is...this." she stuttered while she clenched her fist which was already sweaty.

"I want you, and I want you now!"

Mr. Kashmir pounced on her almost immediately, forcing his lips to hers while he struggled to keep her seat stable. She struggled to push him off but her one arm could not do the magic. In seconds he had his hand in her breasts squeezing them maliciously and eventually tearing her T-shirt apart. She struggled in fear trying hard to push him off while she screamed and then being conscious of her screams, he uses his right hand and forces it down to her mouth.

"Don't waste your time honey! No one will hear you."

Her eyes widened in fear when he suddenly rose and

dragged her to the long couch he had in his office. Not giving her room to breath or scream, he quickly unzips himself and while she tries to drop off the couch to run away, he drags her back and then, he lifts her bogus skirt and slots himself in while she screamed.

His spittle was all over her body, and so was his sweat. Her cloth was in shreds and so was her heart. What had she done to undergo such pain...She watched him zip his trousers and lick his lip in satisfaction while she embraced herself in her torn clothes which reeked of a stench she couldn't bare. The tears refused to roll, but then the obvious pain was in her soul. Her first time, and it had to be rough and sadly, no one came when they heard her scream, no one even knocked!

"Well, Kaneng, or whatever your name is, please leave my office. We are done!"

He sounded so ruthless.

Kaneng wished there was a weapon so she could see him bleed, but, she was too weak and she felt defeat. She rose to her feet slowly, and with no words or will to say anything, she tried to unlock the door that was so hard to reach a few moments ago, and she walked out.

The sun looked red in her eyes; she saw no soul in the mines. Seemed she was left alone to her fate, alone to face the hate. She could not bear the humiliation, seemed like every wind that blew was an eye watching her use her one arm to adjust her torn clothing. But then, she kept walking feeling like a lone miner, with no one or nothing but she was certain that someday, some how she was going to make Mr. Kashmir pay and she prayed for the moment.

The Plantain Boy

CHAPTER ONE

I go go far
Hunger no go catch me
Plantain go yanfu
Na plantain boy I be

It was the month of January, with the roaring wind and the spray of dust and a cold that seems to crust, an alert of harmattan in Abraka, Delta State. Rume laid on the cold. concrete floor with his hands folded behind his head and his eyes faced to the cracking ceiling as tears rolled down his eyes. His chest was heavy with the pain that only his tears could express...a stream of darkness in this one bedroom apartment, illuminated by a dying candle light. His mind wondered around the room with no clarity of what he was searching for. *Why is life so hard?* The sound of a humming mosquito interrupted his thoughts as he clapped in the hope that he had killed it. It made him smile. *How can something this little be so mighty? Causing malaria everywhere!* The thought ceased when he suddenly was drawn to the sound of his mother snoring. It sounded in harmony with a low and then a high, like a choirmaster were giving a signal; he

61

chuckled. He gazed at his mother, in a clad of her wrapper, slapping herself almost instinctively to the sound of humming mosquitoes and then her hands dangling out of the small mattress laid on the floor.

He always wondered what his father looked like. His mother said he was a taxi driver and his name was Julius. She told him the story one warm night while she cut his toe nails.

"Your Papa name na Julius," she said, lost in memories of him. "E dey sit down for that NURTW park well well, and na there we jam wen I wan go Warri. We suppose marry," she paused, sighed, "but things come happen. I get belly, na so I take born you," she continued, somewhat ashamed and not finding the need to extend her story. "As I born you na," she gulped down spittle, "he waka comot. I never see-am since ten years now…for my head maybe he don die but peepo dey talk sey he dey Warri."

Rume did not know what to make of this story. He watched her wrinkled, beautiful face express sadness. She wasn't old, the world made her old, but the lines of beauty existed around her dark skin and at this point, she cared less for male attention.

Rume dwelt on this memory; he didn't feel like lying on the mattress, after such a long sad day. No one bought plantain today; no one even looked his way. *I want to go to school,* he thought as he hugged his body on the concrete floor wondering at the same time why he couldn't sleep. How he, so young, could not seal his eyes to sleep. He sighed. Looking at the dimming candle light, a song began in his head, his favourite Sunday school song, having a piano in sync in the imagination of his mind,

"Doh doh doh Oghene doh! Doh doh doh Oghene doh!

Oghene doh! doh oooo doh! Oghene doh doh ooo doh doh doh!"

He liked the rhythm in his mind, sounded like not just the piano but other instruments playing...the drums, the tambourine and, yes, the *shekere*. He pictured himself dancing to the melody, unconsciously nodding his head in reality and humming at the same time with a smile. Lost in the melody, he squeezed his hands in between his legs and slowly like the dimming light, he faded in sleep.

The voices were growing louder as he walked towards the door, there was a light trying to force its way through the little space left ajar that allowed the voices to be heard. Rume heard his mother's voice, she sounded like she was choking and another familiar voice, a voice of trouble. He ran towards the door and pushing it wide open, he was blinded by the light and felt he was on a cliff and about to fall when he heard a loud thud. He blinked his eyes open. *It was only a dream!* He sighed in relief, but then he turned his head to the thundering voices of mother and landlord exchanging insults. *That was the other voice.* He concurred as he walked towards the door while he watched his skinny mother tie her wrapper over her chest countlessly as she hassled the landlord.

"Water dey here! Eh! Why you go dey come ask me for rent when all the things wey you promise finish no dey the house!! Na this kind yeye house you wan come to dey ask person for rent?! *Shuuoo!*" Rume's mother barked as she moved her body to the sound of her voice.

The Landlord had a stern look.

"Yeye house *abi*?! And you no one pay the rent?! I go bring my boys come for you o madame!! The kind character

63

wey you get bad for your pickin no come dey show yusef anyhow for here! You hear me so! You go give me my money or else…"

"Wetin go happen Landlord?! Wetin you go fit do?!" she dared him.

At this time, the argument seemed to have a pulled a scene as neighbours, rising from their beds, opened their doors to the quarrel and stood with their hands folded or leaning on the door while they watched Rume's mother act all cantankerously and the Landlord matching her.

It was a small compound, houses arranged in no order with a four-foot fence that was deliberately uncompleted as the years have told on it. There were plantain trees on the side, and shrubs scantily placed in edges. Rume watched the eyes around, passersby also stopped to watch the early morning drama. He didn't like it. *Mama always liked drama.* Once she caused a scene when their neighbour, Onoriose, picked her bucket without permission.

"Ono! You wan die *abi*?! Shey na to die dey hungry you? Dem send you come my side?"

Onoriose certainly didn't take it lightly, especially with the mention of death. He brought out her bucket from his room and flung it on her face, which hit her real hard and gave her a deep scar on the jaw.

Mama was enraged. She took off her wrapper, which was the only thing she had on, and rushed towards Onoriose like a rabid dog. The wrestling was dramatic, for a woman with a petite body Onoriose seemed to be her perfect match as he was very skinny and dry skinned, yet, tall. Rume remembered that scene while he watched Mother argue with the landlord. He knew she wasn't going to cease until she ran short of words. It made him wonder if it was for amusement or she was just a nag. He went in, picked his tray of ripe plantain which was all arranged by Mama and passing by he said: "Mama, I dey go." Sadly, she was too engrossed to reply.

CHAPTER TWO

Who say I no go make am o...
Na who talk am!
I go go far far...
Na my yansh from far you go see!

Rume walked under the blazing sun, strolling throw various streets yelling "buy your plantain here! Ripe plantain here!" Seemed no one was listening. The sun was hot, extremely hot, felt like the gates of hell were wide open at that moment. He cleaned his sweat with his ragged torn green shirt, and still called out "buy your ripe plantain!" He was too exhausted to walk further, and no one seemed to want plantain. While he walked down the street, he sighted an uncompleted building, obviously abandoned for ages. Suddenly, his energy was restored and he walked briskly to shade himself from the scorching heat. It did work; the easing breeze that passed through his face from under the shade, made him close his eyes as it felt like cool water spray. Sitting on crushed stones and dry cement from over time, he just couldn't find a reason to rise and walk; he laid there. He looked at his tray of plantain by his side and thought, *person no go fit carry-am*. While he minced those thoughts, his eyes sealed in sleep.

The walk home was tiring, and all through the day, all he sold were two bunches out of five bunches of plantain.

They looked so ripe and juicy, yellow like the sun caressed them, yet, seems the times were just too had for people to buy a bunch for two hundred naira. Rume continued to yell "Buy your ripe plantain!". The dark night was slowing kissing the earth, Rume knew his time outside was overdue. *Only four hundred today* he thought in lamentation, allowing his young mind speculate on the outcome of tomorrow. While slowly making his way home, using his worn out slipper to lift the sand in play as he walked, he though he caught sight of a dark moving figure hiding within the tall grasses. *I don die today!* But then, curiosity overwhelmed him, and instead of running away, he tiptoed towards the figure slowly stretching his hands towards it when his hands unexpectedly got smacked!

"Jesus!" Rume screamed, but surprisingly holding on to the tray of plantain on his head.

"Rume! You no dey see person dey shit? Or you no get nose again?"

"Jehwe! Na you?"

Jehwe was a childhood friend who stayed directly opposite Rume's one bedroom apartment. She and her family owned a mud two bedroom house, roofed with zinc. With a drunk father who always had red eyes, jobless and his clothes smelling like a skunk, and a quiet mother who enjoys her silence above anything as well as her trade in tomato, Jehwe and her younger sister Ese are young ladies with stories. After school, Jehwe and her sister head for the market, making sales in their school uniform. Every day comes with one rude costumer or the next but Jehwe's mother's silence seemed to bring her customers. They call her "a woman of endurance".

Jehwe rose on her feet and picked a ruffled paper lying not too far from her and wiped her bum.

Rume stood away disgusted.

"Why you dey do mouth like person wey no dey shit?" Jehwe chuckled, aware of her mischief.

Rume bowed his head and found himself concentrating instead on the sand which he lifted with his slipper, watching it fly high and float back to the earth. It gave him a smile.

Jehwe lifted her skirt and stepped out of the bush carelessly, unconsciously looking left and right for any one who may be or had been watching and when she walked up to Rume, she hissed.

"Who tell you say make you wait for me now? Eh?!"

Rume sneered at her, while he used his leg to dig deep into the sand, fascinated by the cone shape he was creating.

"Jehwe, make we dey go house."

As they walked home, basking in the sudden cool weather that accompanied the evening, they stared at their age mates, ten-year olds, walking back from school in different school uniforms, and a sudden sadness overcame Rume. But Jehwe waved at those who yelled her name as if it were a must, "Jehwe!", just so the world knows they knew her.

"As u dey waka come, u see some people for road? "asked Jehwe, distracted by her popularity.

"Which people?" Rume asked.

"I see some people wey wear red cap this afternoon. Dem hold cutlass for head dey dance for road. Dem even get de kind gun my papa get for house."

Rume was attentive but he couldn't find the words to reply. They were almost home.

****

Rume was welcomed by the sound of his mother and neighbours speaking in loud voices.

"Na vigilante o! Dem say den kii person for bush," said a neighbour.

"Kii which person?" asked Rune's mother, who was very absorbed in the conversation, folding her hands to listen.

"Sey all these aboki yesterday for bush go kii one boy. Na so dis vigilante wear their cloth and red cap, with cutlass for hand and some carry gun, dey waka, dey demonstrate for road. No be small thing!"

"Na Wa o!" said Rume's mother. "So den go just kii person just like dat?"

"But I hear say Ovie collect money from Fulani peepo make deir cow chop grass and Abraka people no cum gree! Sey the Fulani peepo dey give their cow cassava from farm make dem chop," chipped in another neighbour, clapping her hands simultaneously with her last word.

"E be like sey for Kwale land, una dey take nonsense *abi*?! Whether Ovie eh, whether Ovie collect money from anybody, if indigenes no want, *wahala* go dey! I tell you, *wahala* go dey!" retorted a neighbour who was fixing his bike and suddenly drawn to the conversation.

"The story wey I hear different-o!" said Ono. "Dem say na one old woman wey go farm and e be like sey de Fulani peepo cum warn-am sey make she no cum her farm again...and na cassava farm she get. E be like sey as she no gree hear warning, she enter her farm. The abokis come carry cutlass chase-am, den she con hide for one corner like that since na her land so. She cum carry phone call her pickin and as de boy come reach, di Fulani peepo butcher-am!"

68

"*Iye*!!!" they all chorused.

"And na man oh! E popular for town sef...I don forget 'im name. E get five big shidren," Ono added.

While engrossed in their arguments, Rume and Jehwe said good bye to each other, slapping themselves on the back and waving.

"Mee gwooh" greeted Rume on a general note.

"Vren doh!" was chorused by all immediately, except his mother.

"Mummy, mee gwooh"

"Vren doh!...eh Rume?! U no sell plenty today again *abi?*! Na wa o. Where you dey enter put?"

"Mummy, I enter everywhere wey my leg fit carry me na."

The conversation ended abruptly after Rume handed her the money of all he had sold. She looked at it pitifully, drowned in worries that countered the initial joy she had when conversing with the neighbours. She folded her wrapper and dusted her feet before walking into their room which was wide open. Rume sat outside, watching the fire his mother had made and waiting eagerly for the food. It smelt like yam and peppersoup, *ukodo*. At that moment, it seemed like it was his favourite meal. He smiled at the thought of taking a bite after a very long day.

****

Night and day seemed to have the same weather this very day. All the neighbouring kids camped in front of Rume's house, playing with sand and clapping to whatever song that came to mind. Tuve, Rume's best friend and neighbour, raised the song "Yori Yori" by the music duo, Bracket. Five children, seated in an uncoordinated circle, clapping their hands into the night and singing "I'm with you my Yori Yori" and danced individually into the moonlight, everyone with a style. The joy and laugher in their hearts lingered into the night, as they found more pleasure in raising new songs. Jehwe raised "Mad over you" by Runtown, nodding her head as she imagined the rhythm and instrumentals in her head, mincing words and singing whatever came out, her peers followed suit. Then there came silence as they all walked to the fireplace made by Rume's mother. They sat around it as the night wavered into deep darkness and they all seemed not to want the night to end. They started to talk.

"When I grow up eh...I wan be militant," said Tuve, while he drew abstract designs in the sand with a stick and put it the dying coal, smiling at the burning stick in great achievement. Tuve was born fragile...a good-looking boy with a mother and no father, like Rume. He learned to be strong over the years. He sold "pure water" in the streets but mostly after school and he enjoyed the flatter he received from female students of the Delta State University, Abraka, who are residents and pass compliments like "fine boy!", " why fine boy like this go sell pure water?" This made him feel special, and he was fascinated about grown women that he was swift to call his age mates "small small girls". Rume looked at him when he said what he wanted to become a "militant".

" You know who militants bi?" asked Rume.

"My Uncle for Warri na militant. How I no go know? In house fine eh!" Tuve said, smiling at the thought of it.

Rume had no words. All he knew he wanted was to go to school. He knew that he needed to go. The night passed in silence, with everyone retreating to their homes eventually. Rume walked into his and heard the loud snore of his mother. *Tired* he thought. She seemed to take the same posture as the previous night with her hands dangling out of the mattress. He climbed into the bed and rested quietly by her side.

CHAPTER THREE

I go waka
E go tey
And di world no go see my face
I go tey

It was a dreary morning. Rume lazily rose from bed, dragging his legs through the mattress until he got on his feet.

"Rume!" His mother yelled, her grating voice echoing into the morning.

"Mi gwooh!" He greeted.

"Vren doh," she replied. "You no one wake up before? Plantain fresh this morning-o! I know sey u go sell plenty. Doh. Oya cum wash your face."

Rume walked towards her, dragging his feet with his sleepy eyes, and taking a glance at the seven bunches of fresh plantain arranged on the tray.

"I go chop the remaining *ukodo*."

She sounded awfully nice that morning. Rume hadn't felt her warmth in a long time, her mind seemed to be far and quarrelling was the peak of the day. Her calmness eluded him, felt so rare. He did all he was told and he walked away

71

with a smile, waving his hands at his mother who was excited because the fresh plantain of the day would bring a good harvest.

"Hmmm, make I look for something chop."

****

The market that morning was crowded and rowdy. For an early hour, market men and women were not expected to be out so early. He wondered what was going on. Through the noise and dreary weather of the day he still yelled "buy your ripe plantain!"

"Plantain! Plantain!!" yelled a passenger seated in a car in a motor park, waiting for it to get full. Rume ran towards her before anyone else could.

"This your plantain fine-o! How much?" she inquired.

"Two hundred naira, Ma."

"You no go reduce the price small? Na two I wan buy-o!"

"Okay. Take-am for three hundred."

"De two abi?" she asked

"Yes ma".

The passenger selected from the seven bunches and gave him his money. Rume couldn't hide his joy; it suddenly felt like a good day.

Not too far from the passenger, as he walked across the road, more people called on him and in an hour, he made one thousand and three hundred naira sales. He jumped in excitement, grabbing his tray in his armpit. *Mama go happy*! He walked home joyfully, whistling and moving his head from side to side, he just couldn't wait to show his mother what he had made. The clouds were setting in, and a sudden cold swept his face.

"Na na na na?" he said in surprise.

He wasn't alone in the surprise at the sudden change of weather which felt like the rays of sun were slowly passing through but seemed to be struggling in between the clouds. He looked up to the sky, rain! The thought occurred to him to run home but before he could lift his feet, there was a heavy downpour. The drops of rain hit the ground like stones, with the weight of vengeance. The clouds darkened, the winds were loud like turbulent waves on a sea. Roofs were lifted according to the tune of the wind, with the rain intruding into homes and shops and people taking shelter like an alien had come to slay. Rume couldn't wait for the rain, the empty tiny zinc shop where he found shelter was going to collapse in seconds.

"I go run go house! E no far."

He took a deep breath and watched for the tempo of the rain, it still seem heavier, merciless. Placing his feet like he were on a race track, breathing in and out, he held on tight to his tray and bolted out into the rain. Home suddenly felt so far, he kept running, with the rain standing as a force in his way, too strong to handle, too obvious to avoid. A pole fell ahead. He was certain this wasn't an ordinary weather, it felt cursed. The rain drops sealed his eyes, but he knew home was straight ahead, racing in the middle of the road. Then, he heard a screeching sound and a bright light swiftly approaching, waving uncontrollably from side to side. He watched as the lights sparked through his eyes, deafened by the sound, blinded by the rain and light, weighed by his feet, he found himself on the ground.

****

"Abraka! Abraka!!" yelled Julius, conscious of the changing weather. "E go rain today-o!" He kept called out, slapping the roof of his Vectra vehicle. The rain had started when his car got full.

"Make una bring una money!" he demanded excitedly, motioning with his palm open wide. The car had three women and a man at the back seat and a man and a woman at the front seat, squeezed in like sardine in a can. The journey began with tiny rain drops falling down.

"Dis rain go heavy later-o!" warned a passenger at the back seat. No one seemed to want to contribute to that conversation, the weather felt too soothing to ignore. Those by the window had their heads leaning on the shields or staring outside; there was always bliss in nature.

Julius had his mind on the wheels, reckoning it will only be right to speed up the journey just in case the rain increased. The passengers didn't complain, obviously was a yes! Lucky Dube's track, "Different Colours", was playing on radio, and it brought him memories he couldn't control. *What happened to Ese?...*"Dat fine woman. I no just fit stay with am...hmmm. And she get pickin. What if na my own?! Naaa...how many times we do am! Taaah!" He didn't hear himself say his last word aloud.

"Driver! You well so?" asked the female passenger at the front seat.

He nodded in response and kept driving. Seemed like the rain increased with his speed, as they pass through Osubi, all the way to Eku, passing checkpoints with ease as there were no men of the law to stop and ask "Drop something for pure water Bros!" That actually made Julius smile. The silence that reigned in the taxi was overwhelming, with no topic raised for discussion. The male passenger at the front seat had his phone in his hand, scrolling through Facebook. Others either had their eyes closed or found themselves lost in the weather and the sound of music on the radio. The roads were getting had to see.

"Driver! Put on your light nau! You no see how the place dark! *Hian!*" suggested a passenger with an Igbo accent.

Julius obeyed.

It all seemed too dark not to ignore such an advice or even argue about it. In the dewy weather, the sight of the sign board saying ABRAKA GOLF CLUB, was a consolation that they were close to their destination. The wind was heavy and whistled passed their sealed windows, it seemed like they were alone on the road. Julius kept struggling to clean the windscreen with the hand towel on his dashboard. His arms ached, handling the steering and the windscreen, and the passengers seemed to care less. *Na wa o!* When he thought he had sufficiently wiped the condensation off the windscreen, he reckoned it won't hurt to increase his speed since they were plying the road alone. But the rains in Abraka were beyond their expectations. From a distance they could see the roofs that were raised by the wind and crashed zinc shops, with their parts littering the landscape.

"The rain heavy for here-oo!!" said a worried passenger, obviously afraid of what may occur. "Driver! You sure sey u no go slow down so?"

"Slow down for wetin! Eh?! For wetin!" Julius yelled, turning his head simultaneously with his words. "We don reach already!"

"Take-am easy nau, Oga Driver!" added the female passenger at the front seat.

Julius sneered at her, holding the previous grudge of her not offering to help clean the windscreen while he struggled to do so. Lost in his present emotions and forgetting to clean the dew that re-settling on his windscreen, he did not take sight of the tall pole that had separated the road. It was just too sudden to handle or understand. Julius lost control in a bid to avoid crashing into the pole and he had no clear view of what was ahead, struggled again to clean the windscreen with passengers screaming "Jesus!" and others hurling different curses at him which he remained deaf too. The car was moving from side to side while he tried to clean off the dew...he didn't see the figure running towards him.

****

Ese stood at the entrance of her apartment, looking out for Rume. The rain had ceased and evening was setting in.

"Where this boy dey?"

Getting restless at the possible thought of tragedy, she stared at the damage the rain arranged; the plantain trees looked like a giant foot had stepped on them, neighbours stepping outside to pick their belongings and fix their roofs. Rume still wasn't home. Her heart sunk in worry as she folded her arms in anxiety. Too restless to stand in a place, she tied her wrapper properly and picked another to shield her from the cold. Walking up the street, she saw a figure she was familiar with.

"Ha!"

Her doubts ruled her, walking close and staring.

"Julius!"

His tall frame could not leave her mind, especially with the way he walked with whatever he had in his arms. Looking downwards and wondering what he has in two hands, walking towards her, she half-ran towards him. With immediate sight of what he had in his hands, she paused, as recognition set in.

"Rume!"

She had her hands on her chest.

Two Girls' Stories 1

They call it *burkutu*. A locally brewed drink or beer like they say from malt or millet, made by women in Plateau state. I hated the smell, maybe because I was familiar with it since it was brewed in my neighbourhood but most especially when Father comes home with the smell all over him. He called it "sipping", especially when he hums his way to his bedroom after puking in the living-room and peeing on the same spot. It was so pathetic and repulsive, with the entire house reeking of the stench.

Poor mother, always able to the task...without complaining she keeps a bucket of water and a rag ready for my father's act and cleans his mess after he must have granted her a black eye. She weeps will she cleans, and it always broke my heart to see her so.

I was no exception you see, I had my own share of beatings especially when I request for money for my fees or books.

I was in primary school when all these drama began, about seven years of age. My father worked in a construction company and recalling the situation, I think he was fired. I must confess that my carelessness did not permit to ask my mother what happened but, that day, he returned home with his tie dangling around his neck and his shirt half way unbuttoned with swollen eyes. We had a tradition, I and my father, whenever he returns home, in excitement I jump on him and we twirl around and on days that he is less exhausted he puts me on his back and we run round our living room. This day was different. As he sat on the only three sitter couch in the living room depressed, I was too blind and excited to the signs when I jumped on him. I was perturbed when he literally flung me away and yelled at me. Luckily, I fell on the cane-chair next to the couch. Without uttering a word, he stormed out of the house leaving me surprised and in tears. Behold, my mother saw it all and quickly she came to me and embraced. That day was the advent of our sorrows.

When he returned home that evening we watched him stagger into the living-room reeking from the stench of *burkutu*, then suddenly, he squatted in our midst, slides his trousers and peed. By time we thought it was over he puked almost immediately sitting on his pee in the process. My mother was disgusted by this; she yelled at him and asked what was wrong with him. She did not complete her speech when he picked the brass carved baseball we had on our centre table and struck her face with it. Dear Lord, I had never seen so much blood! She bled from her eyes and cheek. I was so terrified at the sight of this, I was even more shocked when my father yelled at her reminding her that she was a woman and was in no position to speak. I wondered if he did not see her bleed, putting her hand over her left eye which was bleeding profusely. It was a blend of blood and tears. I, on the other hand, was helpless. And, how old was I? Seven! I had no idea on what next to say or do...I could not help Mother. But then I pursued her wherever she went; first, to the bathroom where I watched her was her eyes and then saw her face bewildered by the amount of blood she saw flushing down the sink. And then I followed her to the kitchen where she picked a clean rag and placed it over her eye. Drowsily, she walked her way to the living-room where she played on the couch, tense and in tears. I sat beside her speechless and helpless, unconsciously, tears rolling down my eyes in silence. From that day, my beautiful, petite mother with the most beautiful eyes I wished I had turned one-eyed as that eye slowly failed and so did everything around us.

My world began to change. My perception of life became cold and hatred for my father began to grow, especially those moments he'd call Mother a witch and drag her by her ear to their bedroom and there on, all I hear were her screams in pain.

Mother turned numb with time. Despite all the screaming and yelling, we never had neighbours come to our aid. I even wondered if we had any. When Father begins his routine on Mother, all they do is peep from their windows and lock them when the sounds become unbearable. And when morning comes, and we are passing by to the market, they'll be seated in front of their homes with their hand on their chins and shaking their heads in pretentious pity saying *"eyah... Kai!"* These gestures were repelling; it made me wonder about the battalion of cowards and hypocrites that exist.

Mother was a trader. She sold groceries such as tomatoes, pepper, onions, vegetables and s few grains. Every morning before school, I accompany her to the market, helping her lift her items. The market women were quite friendly. Whenever Mother showed with a black eye, which was routine, they console her bringing her to tears again. I am always hurt at the sight of this, I was tired of seeing Mother cry. And then they'll tell her "such is life" or "that's a woman's plight, you must endure" or "God will take control", but, I wondered, why should we bear this torture? Why must we endure this everlasting agony? My Mother's heart was aching, could no one see?

My share of beatings were seasonal like I said and I was always ready for when it came. It was either I wore two shorts or skirts underneath in case Father decides to use his double-mouthed whip, which he bought solely for myself and Mother, or I screamed abruptly when he decided to slap me, allowing me to run out of the house without being touched further.

However, Father made his molestation a habit, with or without alcohol; in addition, he became slovenly, lazy, bitter and always angry. All he did was sit at home and watch television and demand that Mother puts meat in every meal even days that she was penniless. Whenever he wanted Money from her for his *burkutu*, he'd asked her rudely and insist she handed over to him any money she made during the day. He looked so ugly with an unappealing potbelly and swollen legs. He was unshaven, leaving him with beards that were constantly stained with *burkutu*. He was unpleasant to the sight.

****

Family members did not intervene. I was surprised when Mother said our paternal extended family were aware of the situation but refused to intervene. Always reminding Mother that as a woman she is meant to tolerate and endure such scenarios. My grandmother was even more naive to call it "the pains of womanhood" and emphasising that she went through the same with my grandfather but today he is a changed man.

A changed man indeed! I think old age controlled his actions and would she attest that she is a happy woman?

My grandmother was walking with a stick while my grand father was still agile and still drinking *burkutu* although with no energy to batter my grandmother. The adverse effects on my grandmother were numerous including obvious loneliness. So, Mother seeking her intervention was like a cow meeting a butcher to spare his life.

But in spite of all this pain, and with the years that passed, I appreciated Mother's need to save. She ensured I went to school, not lacking in my fees or books. She had me going to a Day Secondary School, insisting that the sight of me gave her a reason to live. But she impressed upon me taking my education seriously, advising that I should not neglect it like she did, marrying my father immediately after secondary school because she was pregnant with me.

On one of our moments together, I was in JSS3 by then, I observed that she was so depressed, more depressed than she had ever been. I asked her what was the situation and reluctantly, she told me she was pregnant. I was so elated. In my mind I wished for a girl just to have a partner in crime but Mother was not happy. She said she was two months pregnant and while she spoke I saw darkness in her eye and tears began to roll. Then, it occurred to me, what will Father say?

Sadly, my expectations were as I thought. Father looked sternly into Mother's eyes and called her a whore in my presence. He insisted that he never recalled the day nor time that they were affectionate and intimate which coincidentally was true but Mother was his victim of constant rape. Mother teared silently with her hand on her chin as she watched him call her different names and to seal the insults he bestowed upon her, he called her cursed. Hearing that I cried out loud I challenged him for the first time and told him never to say such cruel words to my Mother. He was surprised at my act. Mother quickly scolded me. I wondered why I even uttered a word. Father did not speak surprisingly, instead he rose to his feet and headed for the kitchen and when he came out, we saw him with a knife in his hand. Without thought he shoved me aside and advanced towards Mother, stabbing her in the belly.

I could not believe my eyes...Father didn't too. It all happened in a flash. He shivered when he realized what he'd done, dropping the knife to the floor while he stared at his palm. It seemed like a movie to me as I watched Mother slowly slump to the ground. Swiftly, I rushed to where she was and I embraced her almost unconscious body in tears, suddenly, it occurred to me that there was a neighbouring police station. I dashed out of the house in a hurry still leaving Father in his oblivion and ran to the police station. When I got to the station I was lucky to have met two young bored policemen sleeping on the counter. Quite startled, they were attentive to my summary of the situation and with no waste of time they picked me in their Peugeot wagon, leaving the station locked and went straight to my house. We arrived in time to take Mother to the hospital who, happily, was still conscious. Father on the other hand was beside her when we came and he was numb, looking into his palms and staring at Mother. I cared less what was running through his mind, neither did the police when they arrested him. One of the police men took him to the station while the other accompanied us to the hospital. His name is Officer Yohanna.

By time we got to the hospital that night, we were lucky to find a doctor who quickly attended to Mother and with the help of Officer Yohanna, he ensured she was given immediate attention. He paid for her hospital card at the reception and deposited an amount which I am not aware of till today.

The next day, Officer Must returned in the morning with snacks and a drink for me. It so happens that at that time, I had not heard from the doctors on Mother's situation and so when he came, he looked for anyone to spare us some information but the nurses said they needed a family member, an adult. Officer Yohanna then came to me and asked "do you know your mother's family",

"Yes," I replied.

He then suggested I take him to where they lived so that they could help the situation. Well, luckily I did know where they lived despite seeing them once in a blue moon. On the way to my grandparents I asked about my father.

"He is in shock" he said "and I don't think he will be talking anytime soon."

A part of me was at rest, the other was filled with pity and compassion for my father and then in curiosity I wondered why he had to go this far, a man of laughter and smiles now a man of deep misery.

We got to my grandparents' in time, finding them seated at the veranda of their beautiful home surrounded with numerous flowers enjoying the morning sun. They were so excited to see me, simultaneously asking if I had come to spend the holiday with them. But with the sight of a police man and observing my cloth which was blood stained their eyes widened in worry.

" What is wrong Ami? Why the policeman and why are you stained in blood?" My grandfather asked anxiously awaiting a response. I then narrated the situation to them and how it ended, and before I could conclude, my grand mother began to roll on the floor crying her eyes out.

"I told you *Kitceme...an fada*! I told you not to allow Wurot marry that fool!" My grandmother cried out loud while she kept rolling on the ground struggling with her wrapper in the process.

My grandfather was astounded. He advanced towards my grandmother and cooing a few words I do not recall, he lifts her to her feet while he embraced her.

"Your mother never told us what was happening?" he queried. "The last time she visited and we asked what was wrong with her eye she said she hit it on a pole."

He sounded disheartened, they both were.

Quickly, they locked the house and we left for the hospital. Officer Yohanna did not come along saying he had duties to attend to. Before he left he whispered in my ears "Jesus loves you". I was consoled by this and I did not utter a word. In fact my thank you was at the tip of my tongue.

My grandparents went in search of the doctors and found the one in charge of Mother's case. They emphasised that Mother needed an immediate surgery and explained how lucky she was to be alive but, she lost the baby. We were saddened by the loss of the baby and my grandparents were more furious at my father but we were glad, Mother was conscious. The doctor requested an immediate payment for the surgery to begin. My grandparents had no issue with that, as University lecturers with good payments they had no problem but it was a wonder why such literate people will allow their only child make the mistake of her life which is certainly, not me.

We all sat at the reception of the hospital the entire day with no appetite for food or a bathe. I was still wearing my blood stained dress which I forgot to mention was a white cotton gown. We stuck close to each other in prayer as we waited anxiously for news from the doctor. We saw no one come out of the intensive care unit as we had our eyes transfixed on the door. Eventually, after hours of anticipation, the doctor in care of my mother walked up to us wearing a depressed look. At this moment, tears waited to fall from my eyes; I could not loose Mother, she was all I had and I had to let her know how much I loved her. But then, the doctor's facial appearance was not helping my case. The tears began roll when he said she survived the surgery and she will be fine. I cried with joy and thanksgiving to God. My grandparents were virtually jumping in excitement. We asked if we could see her but the doctor reiterated that she needed a long rest hence we should take the time to eat and have a bath.

I followed my grandparents to their home, where I had a nice warm bath and waited for my grandmother to finish cooking the *gwuate* she hurriedly started making the moment we entered the house. *Gwuate* is a Berom traditional meal on the Plateau, made with lots of spinach and grains called *acha*, with any extra alternative of vegetables or ingredients. My grandmother did not cook hers the regular way, she put some offal in hers which she had in store and spiced it with garlic and ginger. My nostrils had perceived so much of the aroma that I drooled to taste the meal and when I did, I was not disappointed. After we had finished eating, we packaged some for Mother, grandmother did that heartily singing praises while she took the food flask to the car.

By time we arrived at the hospital, Mother was already awake and seated like she was expecting us. I was so elated, seeing my Mother alive again and hearty. She looked so pale and without delay after pleasantries we gave her food to eat. I had never seen her rush a meal before but this day, she did. She ate without pause like a cat on a fish or a dog to food, but...I was happy. We all were happy, laughing in gladness and forgetting our past.

****

It's been fifteen years now and, yes, I am now a mother also, to a boy and a girl. My husband is the best there is and you would not believe who...Officer Yohanna. It felt like we were destined for each other from the beginning. I am a happy wife and mother and Mother is even happier as a grandparent.

I visit Father in jail, secretly. He is still numb though even in his old age. Whenever I visit it is either he owns a black eye or a smashed tooth. It disturbed me to see him this way. Almost all his teeth are gone. I asked the prison guards how come a numb man will undergo such and they confessed that his roommate is a known bully in the prison and they themselves are terrified of him. They said the bully uses Father as his punching bag in rehearsal for whoever he plans to molest in the prison. I then spoke to the head of prisons who said he would make an effort, an effort he never made. After so many years of being pledged guilty, I could not help myself in catering for Father, that love and some good memories still remained, besides, what good is it helping only friends when you could be blessed helping an enemy? He did not deserve to be forgotten. I just wished he knew a woman's worth.

Two Girls' Stories - II

Getting pregnant was not part of the plan. All I wanted was to love Preye and eventually have a family with him. He did not say that I had to change my plans because of a sudden arrangement, a baby! A baby?

I mean I had to bear the pain, embarrassment and shame...all alone. He actually never cared, all he suggested was we had to do something about it and...fast!

I was only sixteen when my world began to turn around. I had this ideology that I would not be in a relationship until I am eighteen or better yet, twenty. My peers were quite intimidating especially when they received letters from their boyfriends from other schools. Being in SS3 without a boyfriend on the outside in a girls' secondary school is a true definition of an alien which I was beginning to feel like since virtually all my friends had one. They felt I was too serious and stiff. A fine girl like me, they said, should not be found lonely or needy, that the men were meant to stoop for me. I usually laughed at this assertion but coupled with the advice I had from my mother about boys I reckoned I stick to my principles. But...Huh! It was so hard.

Before we returned home for our second term holidays, my friends and I had a circle of conversation. During the conversation, one of them sprung a topic...sex. I usually turn automatically deaf during such discussions but, this time, I paid attention. One of my friends began to tell on her first sexual experience which was at the beginning of the term just concluded. I had my hands to my mouth, keeping my thoughts in mind and wondering what sort of indiscipline is this. She gave an explicit description on how she found herself in the boy's apartment and just like the movies, he savagely took off her clothing which she found exciting. She had just turned sixteen, two days before the conversation. The others told their stories too, I wondered if they lied or it was real but I felt like the odd one out.

From that moment, I began to crave the unknown...sex. My friends' experiences filtered my thoughts and principles thus leading to a new decision, I had to have a boyfriend.

By time the holidays began, which was arranged for two weeks, I had already prepared my mind to a selection of any credible boy as boyfriend which certainly will be unknown to my mother. I then remembered there was a boy on my street, Tony, who asked me out once and I gave him the boots, telling him I was too young to date anyone. He was a good looking intelligent chap with sure prospects. I had the hope of seeing him again as I felt I was ready to give it a try. And as fate will have it, we crossed paths again one day when I was helping my mother pack cartons to her restaurant. I was sashaying on the street with cartons in my hands when I heard a familiar voice and behold, it was Tony. Nice guy, he helped me with the cartons and while we walked to my Mother's restaurant which was a stone throw from my house, we talked. In between the conversation he revealed that he would be travelling to the states the next day for his graduate programme in computer engineering. I marvelled at his status, regretting why I never gave him a "yes" when he asked, but then, I was happy for him somewhat cancelling him from my list of prospective boyfriends. But I was glad we met because we had a good conversation and established friendship.

Most of the lessons I had learnt in life started with my mother. As a single parent she taught me to pay less attention to frivolities and have a focus. She was strict and timid on anything that concerns me and it suffocated me. I tried to understand why she had to be so rigid especially when I request to visit my father whom had visited countlessly and all she kept saying was "he is not a good man". As much as I appreciated her, I felt like a bird in a cage despite my age. It was really hard returning a visit from my friends, because I was hypothetically handcuffed to my mother and thus, this made me question if I was truly ready to confront her with my thought of having a boyfriend. The entire holiday was dedicated to helping her and the restaurant, meeting the same faces and undergoing the same routine.

But, on one of those annoying days, I gazed upon a handsome fellow as he walked into our restaurant majestically. While he sat, I had my eyes glued on him and I seemed not to be the only one because he had my mother's waiters staring. Before anyone could approach him, I rushed to his table to take his order. It's eccentric how we connected. It was so natural. We found ourselves having a long talk forgetting his reason of being in the restaurant. I felt my mother's eyes piercing at me from a distance but I didn't flinch. We both got carried away until one of the waitresses pinched me as she passed and giggling to distract the customer. Quickly, I took his order. After he had eaten and he was about leaving, he gave me a tip, told me where he lived and his name. His name is Preye.

Preye was the boy next door, a youth corper from Lagos State according to him. I took an immediate liking to him, felt like love at first sight. We began to meet on the regular fixing our time for whenever he returns from his place of primary assignment. Amusingly, my mother was never aware, she was too exhausted most of the time to figure my whereabouts. I had never had so much excitement. When we meet, it's always sweet with him telling me how his day was and the activities he partakes in, and while he talked we cuddled or played games. I loved hearing him speak but the rendezvous was slowly closing with my holidays coming to an end. But, it didn't stop there. We used the few days I had left judiciously after which we continued in communication through letters. It felt good having the hall mistress call out your name saying you have a letter and I felt even better that it was not coming from a secondary school boy like my friends but, a corper, a graduate! My friends envied my state, especially moments when Preye will slot in some money for me in his letters. I felt married.

Gradually in our letters, we began to build our emotions,

our sexual emotions. We began to exchange sexual notes and it was his teaching actually if not, I was ignorant of such an existence. I yearned for this notes, I even yearned for him more. I found myself calculating with everyday that passed about when my final exams will come to a close and when the final term will end. I kept striking dates on my calendar, a habit I suddenly inculcated and, all I wanted was to be with Preye at whatever cost.

Well, as time will have it, I concluded my secondary school final exams and with out waste of time, I took the first bus home with no final goodbyes from friends. All I heard in my head was "Preye! Preye!! Preye!!!" Like a bell.

When I got home and as soon as I dropped my luggage, my mother was not my priority, after a shower I dashed out of the house looking for Preye whom I met luckily. When we met and embraced, I had never felt such warmth and affection, it was enough to sway me to bed easily without persuasion. Preye was all over me, we opted out on protection because Preye said it will seal our love. He was my first and I certainly did not regret it, in fact, I felt I had a story to tell my friends.

With time, sex became a routine for over two months, and it became an obsession for me. I even marvelled at my being dedicated to helping my mother in her restaurant and still showing that same dedication to Preye. Eventually, my ways changed. The energy I used to have was slowly fading away; weakness was trooping in, I became sluggish and found myself sleeping unconsciously. My chores were suffering and so were my responsibilities. My mother was beginning to notice this and one day, she asked: "you sure say tse-tse fly never bite you?"

I laughed when she said so, like though she were teasing me. I then did not see my menstrual circle after which I began to feel dizzy and then, nausea. The morning sickness hit me unawares one morning when unfortunately my mother was in the bathroom. I rushed to the bathroom and dipping my head to the sink I vomited all I ate the previous day. It felt like my lungs followed suit. By time I was through, my mother was at the entrance of the bathroom door with her hands at akimbo, wearing a stern look.

"What's wrong with you Ella?" she asked gruffly.

I could not tell what was wrong with me, but I know I felt weird.

"Are you pregnant?" she demanded to know.

While she spoke, I stood speechless but then I had to respond.

"No!" I said firmly.

All these eventually got me thinking. *What if I was pregnant? Could my mother be right?* With all these questions in my head I had to look for Preye. When he returned from work that day, I appeared before him perturbed and it got him worried. He was acting all sweet and charming, swaying me to talk and then probably make love.

"Am pregnant," I stuttered.

His eyes widened in surprise.

"Are you sure?" he asked, looking worried almost immediately.

I could not help but tell him the signs I was undergoing and I was versed enough to know such things. He then wanted to assure himself that it could be any other thing but not a baby. While he questioned me, his countenance suddenly changed then, abruptly, he grabbed my harm and insisted we go to the hospital. I was shocked at his sudden change in attitude. He didn't even allow me take permission from my mother. I followed him to the hospital, a private hospital not too far away and we were fortuitous to find a doctor. The doctor attended to us almost immediately and after thirty minutes of waiting, the doctor came with the result. I was pregnant. The doctor asked Preye who he was to me and he was swift to say he was my elder brother. I was too stunned to challenge that.

While we walked out of the hospital, Preye rained on me a variety of insults, accusing me of wanting to cause his downfall and he made a big mistake being with a minor. In my mind I thought *"Minor abi?!...when we were tangoing you never thought I was a minor."* He did not stop grumbling, even on the bus. It was like he was biting or beating himself within and then suddenly he was disgusted by me. On the bus, he ensured that my body did not touch his; he went as far as ensuring someone sat in our midst. The tears that weighed in my eyes I could not hold but yet, I had to control. Then I wondered if Preye would treat me this way, how would my mother react?

By time I got home my mother was awaiting my return.

"Where are you coming from?" she asked angrily.

I stood before her speechless. She repeated the question twice before I had the courage to speak.

"The hospital," I whispered.

Apparently, she heard me and then she went quiet as though she was waiting for more details. I felt my heart plug out while I spoke.

"I am pregnant Mama."

I can't say how it happened but I had never heard my mother scream so loud.

A seventeen year old...eh?!" she kept saying over and over again while tears rolled down her eyes.

"Who is he?" she asked with vengeance.

I told her the pregnancy was Preye's.

Then, she suddenly had an outburst of anger, grabbed my hand as we paced to Preye's house. Luckily, we found him by his doorpost. It seemed he was going away because a bag was beside him while he was struggling to lock his door. My mother slapped him on his back and then she bruised him with her own category of insults.

"You paedophile! You ingrate...You fool! How dare you take advantage of a seventeen year old...are you not wicked?"

Preye wanted to speak, acting all respectful and innocent but before his words could come out my mother had hers out drawing attention from neighbours.

I felt so embarrassed and the same for Preye; he looked like he was going to pee or probably dig the ground and bury himself.

But then my mother did not stop talking, repeating the

same insults, to my surprise she tossed me towards Preye and said he must marry me.

I was shocked. After she had done this display, she walked away with the crowd who came to watch the scene making a tunnel or passage for her.

I stood beside Preye, wondering what next he will do. Not to look callous before the crowd he invited me into his house. By time we got in and he was certain the crowd had disappeared, he revealed his disgusted personality.

"Look!" while pointing his finger at me, "your mother's drama will not work. Nothing will happen between us, you hear me?! If anything will happen it will be an abortion?"

I stared into his eyes when he said this.

"Eh?!" I exclaimed.

"I will not repeat myself Ella. If you no want, no *wahala*. But know that the baby will be your burden to bear!" he yelled.

I cried. He did not even look at me when I cried. That night he said I will not share his bed with him, saying he was disgusted by me and my only alternative for a place to sleep was the floor. I took the offer, and while I laid on the floor, I sobbed with no sleep in my eyes but worry in my heart. I put my hand on my belly and I knew for sure that I was not willing to undergo an abortion, neither was I willing to marry this new monster...but I had to make a choice.

The next day was horrifying. Preye did not look at me. He even kicked me on his way out of his room. My mother, on the other hand, looked at me with disdain when I returned home.

I fell before her in tears begging for her forgiveness and she was not moved. She walked out on me and that was when I realized I was alone on this business.

Later that afternoon, one of my friends came visiting and I was too depressed to attend to her properly but she came with the news of our WAEC result being released and that she saw mine. I asked her the scores and she said I had to visit the school. Luckily, I had a piggy bank and from it I had enough to transport me to school which was a distance.

I did get my result, but what I saw broke my heart more. I had over seven credits in both Maths and English but would I ever enter the university now that I will be having a baby? Does this mean my plans will have to change? And yes, they did have to change.

****

It was hell living with my Mother and, worst of all, tolerating Preye's sudden hatred for me. He had plans of travelling away without completing his service but with my mother's eyes on him, he could not go anywhere. One day, when I was about five months pregnant, Preye came to my Mother and gave her the excuse of his mother being ill and he had to return to Lagos to look after her. After so much reluctance, my mother allowed him go and, believe me, that was the last we saw of him even till the child was three years old. I gave birth to baby boy, a boy I call Paul.

****

Two years passed, with Paul being five and yet Preye had not seen us, let alone send any form of financial aid or support to us. My mother, on the other hand, made my life a living hell. She made my stay and Paul's so uncomfortable with daily complaints and grumbling. I dedicated all my time to the restaurant just to ensure we stayed in peace together, but no, it wasn't enough. It was like the more I tried the more she found fault but I still kept on, all for Paul.

One day, while helping in the restaurant, my mother called me to the corner, "I have tried my child," at this point I wondered what she meant. There and then gruffly, like though I wasn't of her blood, she insisted I leave her house, me and my son. According to her, I am a grown woman and she inhabiting me is intolerable.

My heart almost tore out of my chest when I heard her speak. I could not believe my ears. I fell on my knees, begging her for an opportunity in penance for my wrongs but she refused, saying she could not tolerate me anymore. Knowing my mother, my plea was a waste of time and so I took Paul and with nowhere to go I ended up at the door steps of my father's sister, Aunty Roseline.

Aunty Roseline used to be best friends with my mother but their relationship went sour when my mother took in for her elder brother, who is my father, and Aunty Roseline was a bit disappointed about the situation. So much so that when my Mother came crying to them, like she said, Aunty Roseline did not support her. Rather she walked away. My mother has been bitter towards them and I understand why, but, in repentance for all their wrongs they have come visiting countless times even without welcoming reception from my mother. And, in secret, Aunty Roseline visited me in school. Thus, she was the first person I had in mind and she was more accommodating than I thought. Aunty Roseline, such a wonderful woman and kind to a fault, let's just say her mistakes make her human; I only pray the good Lord grants her her desires, living life alone without family is quite devastating. Nevertheless, she has not changed; she even insisted I put Paul in school but I had no means. In fact, it was my major worry for my son. In her kindness she helped with that, as a civil servant with no one but herself she felt happy spending the money on Paul.

As much as I was enjoying the comfort, I knew I had to find my way. Aunty Roseline was getting used to our company, making me have second thoughts, but I knew I had to leave, felt we were becoming a burden. So, I broke the news to her. She asked where I was going to stay and how was I going to survive alone with a child which, in sincerity, I knew not how but I was willing to try. She was generous enough to give me thirty thousand naira which I used to rent an apartment, a one bedroom apartment.

When we moved in with nothing but a mattress, curtains and a few kitchen utensils given to me by Aunty Roseline, I reckoned that my life has began especially with my son. My certificate became handy and so I went in search of a job. I job hunted for over two weeks. My food was running out and Paul's needs for certain school requirements were on my neck, it was getting tiring but I had to keep moving. Apparently, secondary school certificate owners are assigned to manual jobs and housekeeping, which I opted for. As much as I would have loved to accept offers from men and make free money, my integrity and the upbringing of my child mattered more.

During one of my searches for a housekeeping opportunity, I saw a poster on a pole advertising an opening for a housekeeper. I then took down the location and went in search of the house. My poor boy was with me all the way. Eventually, we found the house, lo and behold it was a friend of my mother's! I was so excited. Her name is Madame Cecilia, a gentle woman although a drunk. It so happens she is a mother of two grown children, a boy and a girl, and I must confess her husband is more of a gossip than a man which could be one of her reasons for having a drinking problem. Immediately she saw me she granted me the opportunity given she was aware of my status and understood that I needed the money. The job entailed me doing chores after which I return to my home in the evening, with a payment of seven thousand naira at the end of the month. As meagre as it was, I said accepted the job.

With everyday that I worked there and bringing Paul along, I never knew Madame Cecilia was watching. One day she came to me and asked after the father of my son.

"Aunty, I have not seen him since the child was born and I have not heard from him either."

She looked at me perplexed.

"That's terrible! That boy is wicked! Don't you know he

lives in this town?"

I was too shocked to respond.I could not believe it.

"Hiaan...Ella! You mean you don't know?" she asked, surprised while I nodded my head in response.

"Ella, Preye is a born and bred Jos boy who coincidentally, his elder sister and I are neighbours, next door neighbours. I see him here on a regular basis."

While she spoke, my belly churned and my heart felt so heavy. I had tears waiting to pour out of my eyes.

Madame Cecilia saw my reaction and then she stopped speaking. She then assured me that she will speak to the sister on my behalf because she is certain she does not know or else she would have been of help as the entire neighbourhood knows her as a kind woman. As much as I needed help, I considered it a stain on my pride but I realized that I had none left, especially when I stare into those innocent eyes of Paul and watch him draw features on the ground that seem to keep him company. I had to deal with whatsoever for him.

****

It took time to eventually meet with Preye's elder sister. And when we finally did after Madame Cecilia had visited her earlier to tell her of my existence. Preye's elder sister was more charming than I thought, so gentle. She swore to me that she never knew of my existence and she would not term me an imposter since the boy is a resemblance of his father. I cried while she spoke and she consoled me. She then assured me of her support and I should come to her whenever I am in need. And honestly, till this day, she has been a comfort, a God sent. Although I am still into housekeeping, I still get support from her. As for Preye, we did get to see again. I was too perplexed to render him a slap; I didn't have the courage to. It was no news however when I learnt he was getting married to a certain lady who was a graduate and works with the civil service. Unfortunately, he is unemployed with nothing to his name. According to the rumour which came from Madame Cecilia, he had engaged the lady for over two years still owing bags of salt yet to be shared and unable to complete his dowry payments. I pitied him. One painful thing though was he did not find the need to connect with his son, he cared less still.

O well, I care less too and let's say my focus is channelled to the proper upbringing of my son. Paul is seven now and I am twenty-four. I still have hope for love and a good man to help me with my son but before that I have plans, and these plans I must achieve.

The Hole

A dreary raining day, with darkness slowly crawling in. Wale thought his day will be revived given the boredom at work and most of all the sadness at home. He and his friends were seated on a round table in the famous LA Tush bar, with their tables decorated with a variety of green and black bottles almost empty. The five of them sat requesting for more from the bar man, Wale sat back with his neck resting on the couch. He sipped his drink, and nodded to every word his friends said. It was like he wasn't listening, what was on his mind were *Why did I get married? What happened to me Agnes? Where did the love go?* He was deaf to the noise and the music at the background. His home was now hell, a roof of silence with no communication. A manager of a construction firm should have it all, at least, all. But his world was crumbling and he thought he'll find a lover in a bottle.

"Guy! Wetin dey do you?" Asked his friend Jairus observing his friend was in silence.

"Nothing." Wale whispered.

"What?!" Jairus asked, straining to hear.

"Nothing!" Wale yelled.

****

The weather was becoming densely cold with the wind blowing uncontrollably and the curtains being lifted high while Agnes struggles to close the windows. It was getting really late and she was becoming so worried, "Where could Wale be?" She had cooked his favourite meal, *egusi* and pounded yam, waiting for him to come home. She was getting tired of the constant arguing and loneliness. They barely had peace to make babies. Five years after marriage, arguing daily about the same things, what were they fighting for? Agnes reckoned she needed peace and she had to win her husband back but where could he be at this time of the night? Where did he go? Does the weather not terrify him? She paced back and forth in the living room while rubbing her arms to warm herself, it did not occur to her to wear a sweater. The power holding company did not seem to do badly themselves as when she thought she was being consoled by the presence of light, she was reminded of her state when it was absent. She yearned to hear a horn and she was willing to run to the gate and open it, she knew a phone call would not help either since whenever she calls he assumes she wants to make trouble. It was getting to 1 am, and in a bid to save her energy and control her anger she falls on a couch.

****

"Mehn..this your silence is questionable-o. What's the matter?" asked a concerned Jairus, while the others were carried away by the girls that passed with their shorts and tights flaunting their assets.

Wale gazed at the ceiling, exhausted, being deaf to his friend's questions. He used his right hand to caress his bald head while he sipped more alcohol.

Jairus was beginning to get tired of repeating his questions and so he assumed his friend needed some space. He then got into the groove with the others, sizing every girl that passed.

Wale still had his head gazing up, listening to his thoughts and reminiscing on memories. Where did they get it wrong? Back at the university they were the envy of everyone, and all were certain they'll end up together. Wherever Wale was, so was Agnes. They both moved like Siamese twins and were happy all the way. How they first met was quite absurd. Wale, a student of business administration, was on his way for lectures when suddenly his sandal cut. He was so embarrassed at this outcome, given he was one of the good-looking boys in class with the most style, and more embarrassed when he realized he'll have to drag his feet. While he walked, dragging his feet, giving the excuse that he hurt his leg to those that asked and to the others that didn't, he suddenly bumped into a lady. She had her books in her hand, which fell to the ground and then in a bid to help her pack her books their heads jammed. "Ouch!" they both exclaimed, massaging their respective heads and then they stared at each other with a smile, and laughed. That was how Wale met Agnes. It was then he observed her tall slender looks and her pretty face. He knew he had to see her again. Amusingly, out of all the rest, she observed he had a broken sandal, without question she brought out a pin from her shirt which she used to close her cleavage and gave him. He was shocked at the gesture but having no idea on what to do, he improvised with the pin and fixed his sandal, just to last awhile. They had a brief conversation after which they exchanged numbers but acknowledging he had to hurry for lectures they ended their talk.

Wale never knew they were classmates. How come he never noticed her? He was surprised when after the class and he was searching for Jairus, there she was, talking to a friend. And that was how their story began, till this day.

They were the story of so many. A popular boy dating a regular girl, sounded like true love. Moments when they were found in corners cuddling or regular outings when they get to stain each other's faces with food causing a scare and the security kick them out. Or, the first day they made love; the sweet sensation that saddled his soul, a feeling he was certain he had had with no one. It just happened on the field during their late night reading at the faculty, no sound mattered just the sound of her moan as he caressed her with her back on the grass, with a mouth watery kiss of her supple lips. They felt nothing, no itch, no scratch but their hands having access to wherever they pleased. And there followed the thrust and loud moan, it was her first time, and he was so gentle enjoying the pleasure and enduring the pain, sweet sweat on a cold evening.

Wale still had his eyes on the ceiling with his eyes sealing while his phone was ringing.

****

Agnes suddenly startled by the crunchy sound woke from her sleep. "Mtchew...it's just a cockroach." She sounded disappointed although did not spare the cockroach's life. She looked at the clock and it was 3.am. She could not handle the wait, nor could she be so patient. Where could he be? She picked her phone, not minding the consequences and dialled his number.

"Oooo...Wale! Please pick up, please pick. I swear I do not want a fight." She kept reiterating the words to herself. But he did not take the call. She grumbled in frustration while tears followed. She sat back on the couch and sobbed, running her fingers through her corn rows. Her heart was heavy and she was certain he was not hurt. Even if she were to search for him in this big city of Abuja, where would she begin? But she was certain he was well, she only wondered if he was with another woman. That frightened her more. She grabbed her hair in jealousy deterring the idea from her mind.

"I'll kill Wale if he cheats on me," she said in ire. "Why isn't he home?" she cried. She picked her phone again and kept calling him, and calling him but, no response. Her frustration was beginning to devour her and then, she made a decision.

****

Wale kept wondering who was calling his name while he flipped his eyes open lazily. It then occurred to him that he was not dreaming when he saw Jairus above him shaking him.

"Am awake, am awake!"

He shrugged.

"Guy, na we close the bar today-o," said one of his friends.

Staggering to get to his feet, Wale then decided to look for his phone.

"O my God!" he shouted.

"What?!" asked Jairus.

Wale opened his eyes in surprise.

"It's three in the morning, and, and my wife left me fifteen missed calls. I got to get home man."

Quickly, he picked his jacket and dashing out without saying good bye to his friends, he rushed to his car and zoomed out of the environment. While he drove, he was perturbed at the number of missed calls Agnes had given him. He did not remember the last time she had called his line, it's usually a text. Something had to be wrong and he had to hurry home to find out. The road was free… 3.am was the time for witches and he was certain he was not going to see any. Suddenly, his car started slowing down.

"No!No!!No!!!" he protested.

He took a look at his gauge and his fuel was topped so he wondered what could be wrong, given he serviced it the previous day. Or could there truly be witches lurking around? Where the car stopped was at the middle of the road. He jumped down and pushed the car slowly onto the pedestrian part of the road. He stood helpless, and opening his car bonnet, he knew the witches probably had him in mind. All that smoke, with him alone on the highway, he only prayed he won't get robbed or worse, killed. It then occurred to him to call his mechanic whom he was certain will come to his aid but may not pick his calls. He tried his phone. Wale dialled his mechanic's line five times until eventually, he picked.

"Oga Wale...I hail o," he answered with a husky, drowsy voice.

"Abeg Yaks...no time for pleasantries. My car jam gbese for road, abeg come help me asap!"

"Wetin happen?" Yaks asked paying more attention.

"Na smoke just dey comot for the engine. I think sey we service the car yesterday, wetin happen?" Wale asked in exasperation and disgust.

"Oga Wale, I no know-o but where you dey, make I come meet you."

Wale in ire described his location to Yaks who was dressing for the situation.

****

"So, wetin do-am?!" Wale asked anxiously.

"Na the carborator Oga, e be like sey my boys no wash am well."

Yaks was sounding apologetic.

Wale looked at his phone to check the time and it was already five in the morning. Luckily, Yaks did some magic to the car, suggesting Wale returns with it to the workshop in the day. They both parted ways with Wale dropping him off at the workshop.

People were beginning to come out, and cars were gradually crowding the road. Wale moved steadily in order to avoid any further drama. Eventually, he got to his gate and horning loudly, the gate man was in time to open the gate.

"Welcome Oga," the gateman said, yawning simultaneously.

"When...thank you. Madame dey?" Wale asked in concern.

The gateman nodded in response.

Wale came down of the care, carefully locking it and resting his jacket on his shoulders. In curiosity he wondered why Agnes left him that many calls.

The house was unusually quiet, with the flowers lying asleep from the previous wind. He strained his ears to listen to any possible sound probably from the backyard or kitchen. He knocked on the door, which surprisingly wasn't locked, it opened easily. After dropping his jacket on the couch and scanning round, his attention was drawn to the dinning table where he sighted a couple of plates and two well-covered golden-glazed dish bowls. He walked towards the table and opening the bowls he smiled. *Is this why she was calling me?* It was a long time Agnes showed such a gesture; he knew she wanted to advocate for peace. He immediately felt bad not being present to devour the meal which looked so delicious and, it was his favourite! He knew he had to respond to this.

"Agiii!" He called out. He ran up the stairs heading for the guest room which she adapted as hers, "Agii!" He kept calling but still, silence. She wasn't in the guest room, neither was she in the master bedroom which is theirs, so where could she be?

The first thought that occurred to him was probably she left the house, but searching her wardrobe and possessions everything seemed to be in place. It didn't feel right. He searched under every bed and closet. He went to the backyard, searching the rooms and environ but still no sign of Agnes. Where could she be? Suddenly, it occurred to him to try her cell phone. He dialled her number and then he heard the phone ring from a distance. Following the sound as he kept dialling consistently, he found himself heading towards the bathroom in the master bedroom. Opening the door, he was welcomed by a pool of flowing water from the bath all over the floor. The water seemed to have a tint of blood in its blend. His heart was beginning to skip a beat, praying not to encounter the worst, then, he pulled the curtain around the bathtub and there was Agnes in a pool of water, drenched with blood dripping from her slit wrist. She looked so white with her eyes open wide and long gone. Wale, lost and confused, screamed in pain while he struggled to bring out her naked body from the bathtub. He grabbed her, holding her tight to his chest as he rowed back and forth shedding tears he never shed.

"Agiii...Agiii" he wailed.

For The Sake of Hope

The cold breeze swept past their skins as they watched the rains fall, sheltering under a zinc shop. It is like with every rain drop they saw a future, none that any could see but just their hearts as they plead. Tattered clothes with no shoes and their bowls in hand all empty, and so was the zinc shop, very empty and the rain was beginning to enter from beneath. They lifted their legs off the ground, leaning on the zinc as they climbed their way up, all to avoid the cold water from touching the soles of their feet. It was no surprise however when the zinc shop began to shake and their hearts were in line. Tears could not roll even with the fear of possibly spending the night without a shelter, they knew there was always a way, all they waited for was a brighter day.

Lahu was only seven when his mother died. It was so unfortunate when his father, Mr. Uku could not allow his moment of mourning to pass before taking a second wife, Titi. During her stay in the house, Titi ensured that every spoon of food was accounted for especially that consumed by Lahu. She had a way of pretending in Mr. Uku's presence acting all caring towards Lahu. The poor boy could not express himself, even moments when she banged his head hard on the walls of the house when he failed to wash his

114

plate after a meal leaving scars on his head which when his father returned from work and asked, the quick response was "he fell!". Lahu drowned in silence with little or no words to express himself, he wondered if his father will believe him.

Days in school were even harder, with him being all timid, feeling like a reject. His teachers wondered what he was going through and sadly, Titi was saddled with the responsibility of picking him after school. Whenever she does, she is swift to slap him on the head or back for a dirty sock or shirt, saying "I no be your mama-o! You keep getting all your things dirty, very soon you go start to dey wash your clothes."

Lahu never understood tears, whenever she comes to pick him with this attitude and he is certain his peers are close, he raises his head high. A wonder how a child could feel.

In all his silent moments, Lahu will wish for his mother's presence. He never understood death, his young heart could not tell but he knew his mother was no more and if she was around, Titi wouldn't be here. He would have eaten to his satisfaction, he would have played with his friends heartily and have dirty clothes, he would have played with his mother and tell her who farted in school today and who pooed in his pants, he knows he would have smiled. Now, his smiles had come to an end, and, worst of all, he had lost touch with his father. His father seemed to be obsessed with Titi's presence and whatever she said remained. He wanted to run away, just like Snow White did from the hands of her wicked step-mother in the cartoon. And so, one evening when Mr Uku and Titi went to visit their next door neighbour who lost a relative, he picked his school bag, stuffed a few clothes and shoes plus a loaf of bread, and he left.

****

Walking that night, in the lonely streets of Tor, Lahu watched the market women with their lanterns struggle for customers and people swiftly walking to their homes. The weather was cold, and there he thought *where will I sleep? Should I go back home?! No. Aunty Titi will kill me.* He walked, determined that he would find a way and if none he'll lie on the street with his bag as his pillow. He kept walking and observing. He was almost carried away when he bumped into a tall fellow dressed in black "You no know your road again?!" He asked gruffly with a deep husky voice. His breath smelt like burnt leaves and even in the dark his eyes reflected red.

Lahu was terrified and he stuttered trying to mumble out some words.

"Your Mama know sey u dey outside?" the man asked, still looking sternly into his eyes.

Lahu knew he had to leave and so without thought he brushed past the tall fellow who tried to drag him back with his bag, and ran. The further he walked, the less people he saw until he came to a bridge. It was an uncompleted bridge with planks still lying around and there he felt was the perfect place to spend the night. He sat beneath the bridge, gazing at the stars and wearing a soft smile, a smile he lost when his mother died. While he looked at constellation of stars in admiration he suddenly heard a cough. He was startled and instead of curbing in his fear he walked quietly towards the direction of the cough as it was persistent. And as he drew close to the sound he saw a boy of his age, shivering from the cold, holding himself and rowing back and forth. His clothes were torn, and he had no shoes on his feet. In his hair was so much dirt, and he stank from afar. Lahu was drawn to this boy. Swiftly without the boy noticing him, he picked his bag and came to where the boy was walking slowly towards him.

"Hi!" He said, being careful.

The boy looked at him, taking full notice of him.

"Take this shirt, you're cold."

The boy collected it with no hesitation, wearing it almost immediately.

"I bet you're hungry too, cause I am."

Lahu smiled while he brought out the loaf of bread he had stuffed in his bag. The boy smiled accordingly and they shared the bread. As they ate, Lahu asked "what's your name? Mine is Lahu."

The boy looked at Lahu as though he wanted to be certain to trust him and then he said "Rabiu".

****

That was the day Rabiu and Lahu began their friendship. Two seven-year old boys walking mindfully on the streets of Tor and beyond…eating whatever scrap they are provided with and begging for alms from whoever decides to be overtly generous. They seemed to have forgotten their homes and lives especially Rabiu who had his briefly. Rabiu's parents, Mr and Mrs Haruna were both teachers. They both died in one day in a car accident that involved Rabiu as well, he was six years of age, but he survived. The poor boy wakes up with the thought of the tragic scene, appearing as a recurrent nightmare filling him with guilt and illusions of how he killed them because he was a stubborn son or how he could have saved them. His little mind seemed to be above his age. Unfortunately, none of his relatives was willing to cater for him after the loss of his parents. Like a ping pong he moved from one relative to the next until he was seven years old. He was tired of the hand exchange, thus one day, he made a decision to be his own man and leave the house.

Lahu and Rabiu were well known about. With women sending them on various errands as well as certain shop owners. They were both known for their integrity and diligence. But yet, no one knew where they laid their heads, or if they have ever pulled off their shoes because of the weather. They were both always looking white like stains of dust and their clothes were beginning to have holes , so were their shoes.

They could not tell if their actions were right or wrong but they knew they smiled. Especially days when passers-by decide to be generous, Lahu always suggest they buy ice cream sold on bicycles, and there they would share the scoop they buy for twenty naira. In fact, other boys, the *almajiris* in particular also dive into the scoop. They ran around parks heartily like birds in the field, being hungry skips their minds sometimes. Yet, the pleasure of being free from sadness, in spite of hunger, made their little minds rejoice in liberation. Although, the sad days do come, days when they have their bowls in their hands and begging for alms or when some of the market women decide to give them some leftover meal in the same bowl they beg in, licking every corner of their hand after licking the bowl as well. Who taught them the skills of survival? You'll wonder, but that's a gift of every human being. People usually shove them aside, pushing them as far as the main road. They had the feeling that a person with a soft face is easier to approach; sadly, most of their cases were unfriendly. One time they held a man by his garment on both sides and then he turned around and slapped Rabiu real hard since he was closer. Lahu and Rabiu both withdrew, with tears in their eyes wondering why he had to go that far.

Meanwhile, Lahu's parents were searching for him. It had been over eight months since they last saw him and went as far as reporting him as missing and putting posters on walls. Titi pretended to empathize every step of the way, trying to console her devastated husband who was beginning to feel guilty for neglecting his son. His routine prayer was for the boy to be alive, with the hope that he was not stolen from the house. Nothing Titi said could avert Mr. Uku's emotions. It even affected his work. In his heart he knew, his son was alive waiting for something new.

Lahu on the other hand did not feel like he had missed a

thing. He found a new friend in Rabiu and whatever the travails they were sure to overcome, such thoughts in little minds.

The raining season, with its pros and cons, made their struggle harder even worst with no shelter. In spite of the errands they undergo none saw it fit to know where they lived. The bridge where they first met was becoming a habitant for dirt and dustbin. They had to change base and luckily they found an abandoned zinc shop not too far from the bridge. Although the space was a little tight, they found a way to squeeze their little bodies and cover themselves with their surviving clothes. One night, after they both returned, extremely exhausted from work and play, a man moving around the zinc shop suddenly decided to ease himself. He was obviously drunk, staggering back and forth with his urine doing the same, splashing all around like a host with water. The boys were terrified. Again, he decided to lean on the zinc shop which was slowly tilting to smoke his cigar. He lit the cigar and while he smoked, nature's messenger passed it through the nostrils of Lahu and Rabiu who were already finding it hard to sleep. Suddenly, Rabiu began to cough, and cough uncontrollably. He coughed out so loud that Lahu was beginning to fidget in fear meanwhile the man with the cigar unaware of his environment kept smoking his cigar. Rabiu was slowly suffocating and coughing out simultaneously and all Lahu could do was stare in worry with tears already rolling, helpless to the situation.

"Rabiu! Rabiu!!" he kept calling.

Rabiu had his hand to his throat while he tried to calm himself with his eyes already bulging out. Lahu unconsciously, picked a sachet of water they had on the reserve and forced it down Rabiu's throat. Rabiu stopped coughing, laying his head down and trying to catch his breath. Lahu smiled, his friend was not going to die. The silly fellow still had his back on the zinc shop looking around as though he did not want to be caught. Then, Lahu found the courage to do something adventurous knowing the man was drunk. He stepped out of the zinc shop, picked a large stick that was lying on the ground, walked towards the direction of the man and observing he was a bit skinny and weak, he did not feel intimidated. And from behind he hit the head of the man so hard that when he turned around dazed and seeing Lahu wielding his stick he yelled "ghost!," and took to his heels. Lahu smiled at his mischief and returned to check his friend.

And then came the rain that night that took their shelter away. They watched the drops fall steadily, then heavily. And with every drop they saw hope, until in it's heavy state they began to battle with the sizzling cold rain water and how suddenly they were in a pool of water in their shelter. In a bid to escape, their tilted zinc shop eventually fell to the ground slowly taken away by the flood. They shivered in the cold running with the rain heavily pouring on them, seeking for a place to hide. All their available cloths and items were swept away by the flood and certainly they could not hunt for them under the wild weather. They kept running, with the rain drops blinding their eyes, and then, they sighted the bridge.

"Let's stay under the bridge!" Rabiu suggested, with them forgetting it was now a dustbin. Quickly, they took shelter under the uncompleted bridge, under intense cold without any means of warmth. They shivered like chickens under the cold, trying real hard to stay away from the dustbin and bearing the intolerable stench. They sat in silence, watching the rain fall non-stop and not even knowing when sleep came.

The long awaited morning came, with the sun shining bright and Lahu and Rabiu lying fast asleep next to each other. They felt the heat on their skins and then voices that echoed in their ears. Lahu was suddenly awoken by a caress on his head. He smiled, still half awake with the caress reminding him of his mother, until he fully opened his eyes and saw what he did not wish for, his father. Mr. Uku had tears in his eyes when he saw what had become of his son, dressed in tattered clothes and looking very thin and malnourished. He grabbed his boy, hugging him tight to his chest. Behind them was a crowd of watchers, carried away by the emotional moment, a reminder of the prodigal son. Lahu was not too keen about his father's presence but he returned the affection all the same. Rabiu on the other hand, waking up sluggishly is startled by the crowd and the fellow hugging Lahu in tears. He wanted to ask questions but he was also carried away by the moment. Mr Uku was holding on to his son, still awed by the moment, "why did you leave home Lahu, why?" He cried. Lahu was too dumbfounded to reply, thinking of the words, suddenly, he found the words.

"Aunty Titi hates me. I want Mummy!"

That was when his tears began to roll.

Mr Uku was now helpless, searching for the words to console his son.

"Come home with me," he said.

"No!" Replied Lahu hesitantly.

"Why?...why Lahu?!"

"If Aunty Titi is still living with us, I don't want to go home," Lahu replied boldy.

Mr Uku then had a loud laugh that sounded somewhat sarcastic with the crowd, Lahu and Rabiu confused at his display.

"Titi is gone Lahu, she is gone. We had a divorce recently. I realized that she was not a good woman."

Lahu smiled and looked into his father's eyes in curiosity waiting for what may have been his reason for divorcing Titi but his father only returned the smile heartily.

"So, can we go home now?! And I promise never to abandon you again."

Lahu smiled and then rose to his feet with the crowd cheering at the reunion of father and son. And while they were about leaving with Mr. Uku's hands on Lahu's shoulders being all carried away, Lahu remembered he had forgot something.

"Wait!"

He stopped himself and his father from moving any further, walked back to the bridge and stretched his hand to an already perturbed Rabiu on whose face was an obvious sorrow. When he saw the stretched hand, he wore a very large grin and holding their hands together they walked back to Mr. Uku who was still in the dark of what was going on.

"Daddy, this is Rabiu and he is my friend. Can he come with us?"

Lahu had the glittery teary eyes that one could not say no to and without thought Mr. Uku willingly said "Yes". Everyone at the scene was all so happy, watching Mr Uku and the boys walk away in joy and love, forgetting their day's activities.

"How did you find me, dad?" Lahu asked while they walked away.

"I was walking down this street this morning, totally worried about you even after the storm yesterday, and while I walked with a poster of you in my hands I met a skinny fellow whom when he saw your picture he screamed "ghost!". I then tried to persuade him to reveal where he had seen you given how frightened he was and then he pointed towards the direction of the bridge."

Lahu and Rabiu chuckled knowing already who the fellow was while Mr Uku kept looking at them in curiosity lost in their mischief.

That of a Deadman

I opened my eyes to a new world, something didn't feel right. My family were all in tears around me. I wondered why they were in tears; I touched them but they didn't feel me, it was like I was a light passing through bodies; none could see me, even when I screamed out their names, none could hear me and that was when I realized, I was dead.

I knew death was coming for me, could not say when. Honestly, I think I needed the rest but I wished it had come later but...am gone. Being sixty and having to work your entire life without stress was quite strenuous for me, and with my kind of heart, I could not let anyone go hungry. I had the habit of bringing relatives to stay in my home, feeding and catering for them even more than my children, relatives that now want to own what is rightfully for my children.

I had five wives during my life time. The first, whose name was Katmwa, gave me a son called Tyrus, my first-born and a drunk. The second was called Mary, a wonderful beautiful woman who helped me build the empire I had. She gave me seven children, four boys - Kelvin, Rotkang, Kichime, Sylvanus - and three girls, Rita, who was her firstborn, Rit and Kermun. The third wife, the most troublesome of them all who I think I married because of her butt, Rosemary, she gave me five children; three boys, Anthony, Stanley and Yilji who was my last child and the girls are Fari and Martha. The fourth wife, Joselyn, who was a Ghanaian, gave me no child. She felt so bad about that that she left, just like that. And the last wife, her name was Macifa, my brother's wife whom I inherited as well as his troubles. She gave me a son and two daughters, the boy I called Babs and the two girls Victoria and Bet. Macifa came into my home with her sons, my nephews whom I adapted as mine, Tare and Bikos. I loved women, I could not help myself. I had concubines as well who gave me children, some I didn't see. A man with such influence and wealth as myself had enough to spread and share.

All my life, I built edifices and estates, making myself influential and important, being all powerful, all for my family, a family I got to know their true identities the day I died. Such hypocrites I lived with, all pretending to be at my service only to waste what I had suffered to build. It's like many were patiently waiting for me to die. For what? My sweat? Now I roll in my grave watching them kill themselves for vanity, worthless possessions, lazy greedy fools! Well, being dead does not stop me from revealing my disappointments even at this moment that I roll in my grave highly aggrieved. I even wished I had fingers to bite.

I looked at all of them dressed in black for my funeral, apparently I was more significant than I thought, with different dignitaries attending my funeral. I watched fake and real tears roll; I watched a few laugh and smile at my demise. One went as far as spitting beside my casket when the crowd had departed. I watched them all. Katmwa and Mary seemed to be the only women who missed me. They cried and they embraced each other while they did. Mary I empathized with. I wished I could console her especially with the way I treated her…I wonder why she still loves me. The other wives did the work of what I call a crying choir, pretending to tie their wrappers endlessly and rolling on the floor with no purpose. I was entertained yet, furious.

My children did not disappoint me, all the men held back their tears and the women, well, I could not blame them, I did not have that much of a connection with them. I had it though with Rita and Rit. Rita cried like a widow, she adored me. Rit, on the other hand, my precious one, had her eyes almost popping out surprised I was gone because she came previously to visit me with her family. I always wondered why she had to get married so early when I had so much planned for her, especially to a troublesome fellow whom I did not like. I was quite irritated by him. Rufus is his name. I considered him way older than she was and he was overly dramatic, taking everything by force. I marvelled at how she coped. But, I got to know why she left so early; she was not happy with the way I treated her mother, and how I never intervened when the other wives were rude to her. I understood.

It was not long when they dropped me six feet that they began to share my properties. According to my tradition, the Ngas people of Plateau state, when a man dies the women do not have a share in properties but possessions and so it was done. I had not yet turned to dust when the girls shared everything in my room between themselves, from the ceiling to the floor. The boys on the other hand, the boys, huh! They are still fighting for the properties till this day. My boys, it disturbed me that they never learnt much from me. I tried to fit them into different schools which they voluntarily withdrew from telling me it's not their ambition. Ambition my bones! They are all hungry now with no life, with their children at the mercy of others. All they wait for is when to sell the next available property which is known as mine.

Tyrus did not live long enough to share in the properties; he was hit by a car while trying to cross a highway, drunk. Kelvin was now the man of the house, if not for tradition, Rita would have been in charge.

Kelvin, my boy, its just ironic that he has my heart and not my wisdom! He was the only one amongst my sons who accompanied me to the farm and did the things traditional men should do, what baffled me was his neglect for education. He was more interested in politics like a traditional ruler, but I tried to inspire him and make him realize that education will render him more power even as a traditional ruler but, it was futile.

None of my sons made me proud, probably Anthony who became a priest and Babs who became an immigration officer. Anthony disappoints me though, such arrogance from a priest. Makes me wonder what is going on in the seminary or was it me? He is extremely arrogant and rude and I am appalled by his actions mostly against his siblings.

Rotkang, Kitchime and Sylvanus, on the other hand,

played out like I thought. Rotkang aspired to be a footballer but lost his way, don't know how but I watch him hallucinate daily and he has no certificate to aid him. Kitchime, the rebel, my soul cries for him, such a good heart but no wisdom, neither does he own a certificate…always bent on alcohol and self pity. And then Sylvanus, my selfish boy, consequences of being the last child of his mother, with no certificate to his credit but I like his faith…he forgets reality.

I was more perturbed by Macifa though in marrying her, I thought I was helping my late brother but then I got carried away by lust and her beauty. I never knew she was so diabolic and evil. The houses I built and she met, houses that had the sweat of myself, Katmwa and Mary before I brought her to me home, are the same houses that no one has access to except her children. I just can't help myself but laugh…that is, if I could be heard.

Did I mention I had a will? I did write a will, giving everyone what was due to him or her, greed did not allow them hold on to what they were given. Macifa ensured that she maintained her stay in my family compound, a compound of houses which I built, giving every wife an apartment with her children. When I died, Macifa moved into the house which I claimed as mine, and was the largest and prettiest. She and her children were known trouble makers and evil moulders concocting a lot of stories and drama. My sanctity became a coven. My room was locked by her for over twenty years with no one having access to the room, she was hiding something. Sadly, being dead I can't say all. Yet, I feared what evil she had propagated in my home, a home I had in control when I was alive, a home that was in order. It appears she was waiting for my death and it came in good time.

****

Everyone has an interesting way of saying how they want to die. I know a few friends who said they'll prefer that they die in a car crash, one said from tapping palm wine, another said while devouring a variety of meat and one said by the gun or on top of a woman. Such interesting ways, but, it so happens that I am a man of peace, I wanted to die in my sleep and truly I must confess that God answers prayers...my wish was granted to me. I died of a heart attack. Before I departed, the doctors said my heart was surrounded by cholesterol, but, who cares? I loved eggs and so what? I made sure that I ate six eggs daily, none knew why but it was no addiction. Just plain pleasure! Still, I knew that being alive was a necessity but I was beginning to withdraw from the world, especially when I began to see people for who they were.

I was a dog lover, I had this dog I called Buzz, a male Alsatian. That dog was more loyal to me than I was to myself. Whenever he understood that I was lonely or sad, it'll cuddle up to me, wag his tail and lick my face just to make me smile, and it always worked. One time, I had to travel to the states, I could not trust anyone to look out for Buzz since all were thinking of themselves and so, I took him to a friend of mine, Alfred, a white man from Sweden. He loved Buzz and Buzz was comfortable with him; and that was how I left Buzz in safe hands for over a month until I returned. When I returned home, the first place I went to was Alfred's, and there was Buzz already missing me. No one has ever been that excited to see me, Buzz cried and hopped on me, barking endlessly in joy. In life he showed me loyalty and so he did in death, as it could not take my loss. Buzz slowly faded away, not eating or drinking, it joined me a week later in the grave dying of a broken heart.

Buzz was not alone in that loyalty, so was Mary, my second wife. After my death, she took nothing of mine, even those that we worked hard for together, she immediately retired to the village to remain in the village family house till she died. She lived like a true widow, and what devastated me more was in spite of her goodness her children were foolish enough to neglect her. They were all blinded by greed and responsibility, deaf to her calls and needs when she ensured they had a better living than any of the children I had. I must confess, I even envied the kind of love and attention she gave them but, she did not stop. Amongst her children, Rit was her soul mate, they were a true definition of mother and daughter, but, Rit did not have a stable life, with the children coming in and her husband unemployed, the burdens did not let her share but Mary understood.

Katmwa on the other hand passed away a year after me and seven years before Mary, she was quite aggressive, one of the qualities that attracted me to her and she was good to me. Just unfortunate she had a child, and that only child turned out to be a drunk, dying a few months after her. But, it worried me, when I was alive that she had a certain level of natural dislike for Kelvin. I remember one encounter when my elder brother, Kaka, had to intervene. Katmwa had the habit of pouring her anger on Kelvin, hitting him mercilessly on the head for no reason and the boy was between the age of seventeen and eighteen then. In my tradition, which if I am not mistaken is a general notion, when you hit someone mercilessly on the head, your intention is to kill the person and that's what we assume about Katmwa. And out of respect for Katmwa, being the first wife, Mary did not interfere, nor did I. But, one day my brother, Kaka, did. He came visiting me one day and then he saw what Katmwa was doing to Kelvin. Quickly he stopped her and insisted Kelvin stay with him. It was not until nine months later that Kaka died and it troubled Kelvin for long, that much that he felt responsible for Kaka's five sons even more than his brothers. But, at the end, the five boys did nothing but betray him over my properties.

I gathered so much wealth, for what? My children do not see eye to eye anymore. They speak to each other with disdain and bitterness all because of vanity. Poor Kelvin, I get confused though...is he an advocate of peace or is he being selfish? I mean, he tries to control the situation, make things right even with no one listening, go as far as calling himself names to make his siblings feel sober but when it comes to getting his share from any properties sold, he takes a lion share. Well, I understand that because he has major responsibilities and he is so innocuous, too extreme for me. My house has fallen apart under his watch; he seems to have left all to chance and fate. However, I must commend his strength, coping with accusations of being a ritualist, handling my concubines and their children whom I certainly dropped a share for and with relatives who feel they deserve a share of my properties despite all I did for them when I was alive.

Rosemary, Rosemary, Rosemary, that woman was hell in human form. I watched her molest and harass the older wives and said nothing. It was like I was hexed, I usually am mute when it comes to her, and I favour her the most. I won't call her the favourite but she had my attention. She had a habit of inviting her relatives which she makes me responsible for and then allows them disrespect whomever they please. Almost all her relatives who visited were thieves. Each stole whatever their hands could grab. One of her relatives whose name I could not forget, Jaba, she stayed under my care for a month with me paying her school bills, which I am certain she did not go to, as well as her personal needs. Rit, while under my roof, came to me complaining that the gold chain I bought her from Italy and the clothes as well were stolen by Jaba. I was shocked. Rit explained how it happened; when she had returned from school that day dressed in the cloth I bought for her and the gold chain, she undressed to go have a bath in the bathroom which was outside only to return to realize her clothes and the jewellery were stolen. She got to know that they were stolen by Jaba, when one of my relatives informed her that they saw Jaba entering her room. Rit went hunting Jaba all over, even as far as her family house but did not find her and that was when she resorted to me. What could I do? I remained silent on the issue and, amusingly, I did not see Jaba even till my dying days.

Well, it's been twenty years since I have been gone. In twenty years I watched them sell my four estates, two hotels and a club, three plots of land as well. And now, they want to sell the house in which I lived, the compound where I built as my sanctity. I pity them. They do not even have houses of their own; they are all blinded for more without cherishing the bare necessities. I wished I had the power to stop them from selling the compound of houses but I can't, am dead!

Masifa just died recently, but I haven't seen her. She went blind and lived in torture but this still did not seal her lips. I must confess that I failed not to have left a business or hobby for her. Maybe her emotions and steaming jealousy for no reason would have been channelled and there might have been peace. All this village women, they had a way of being traditionally extreme, hence one reason why I appreciated Joselyn. She was so sweet. She was prostitute with whom I had a wild sensation; I just had to marry her. She was truly independent, came to me when she was extremely broke. And she was quite friendly to all, but she was frustrated by her inability to give me a child. I felt bad but I already had too many to look after. She felt it was necessary just to have a bond. I was quite careless with her and am sure that's why she left with no farewell. Yet, she attended my funeral.

As for my friends, it seemed a number of them wanted my wives, especially Rosemary. That butt was large and a full distraction. I am certain that's how she got the HIV virus.

Those friends of mine enjoyed levity. It's just so sad that some of them are still alive. In spite of their selfish ways, they were loyal to me for their own purposes. But, it didn't matter...I left them to fate.

My story ends here. I just had to voice my agony and regret, reminding me of the parable of Christ about the man who stacked his barn. I wasn't proud, that's for sure but I did not rest...all I did was gather till the day I died and now, now they are all lost. Now, I await the resurrection. I just pray am found worthy and I also pray that my children will open their eyes before it's too late.

The Man of god

The hard times in the country makes a true friend hard to ask. Begging for a livelihood is as well as serving your soul to the devil in a silver plate. Tunji felt that way as he lay on his spring mattress gazing up to the ceiling, in his very empty room. The clothes that hung on the wall were worn out, and the wall itself was wet from the weather. His pot which was beside him was empty and so was his world. He refused to tear, the feeling of being a man does not permit him to do so. He had no food to eat, and no life to live. The jobs these days are so hard to come by, and that he could attest to as he has tried countlessly to find one, even house boys are given no room. Being a secondary school graduate, he assumed that he need not try to further his education, as it was not his desire and even with the knowledge of so called wealthy men not having to go through tertiary education to be who they are, Tunji felt he could be that way, a hustler! He had run out of options, and so also money and food. "What can I do?!" He thought, still gazing in worry. He thought by this time as a thirty year old, he would have had a life, waking up in the morning like every individual to go to their place of work or better yet taking his time to attend to his business, his business! The thought of owning his own business made his heart skip beats. But, life had provided him with an alternative which is a choice.

Previously, he met his classmate, Emeka, the dullest fellow back then in secondary school, all dressed in suit and tie, driving pass in his SUV until he saw Tunji.

"Tunji my guy! Is this you?"

Initially, Tunji had pretended not to have seen him because he was in a shirt he had won the entire week and was standing by a woman selling *akara*.

"Bros, who you be?" he questioned.

Emeka was a bit taken aback but that did not prevent him from introducing himself.

"You no remember me guy? Emeka na, Emeka from Boys Secondary School Kuru, for Jos."

Tunji then blinked in pretence and kept scratching his head to remember him.

"O! Emeka! Its good to see you-o Bros! Longest time. How u dey?"

"I dey o my brother, God has been faithful."

"I see you are rocking life-o bros. where do you work?!" Tunji asked with a spike of arrogance as he felt his state should not permit disrespect.

"Bros, I dey bank-o! I am the accountant in Zenith Bank in Jos, the one for terminus. Wetin you dey do?" Tunji wondered how he was going to avert the question.

"Bros, it's been awhile-o! You money makers eh! Bros, sort me something na," he chuckled.

Emeka not understanding the situation, slips his hands into his pocket and removes five thousand naira. Tunji grabs the money in a hurry without it being handed to him. Emeka laughs over it and they part ways.

Tunji watched Emeka drive off and wondered if it was the same boy who everyone considered as a dull one? He wondered the miracle that must have taken place in his life and what could have Emeka done to become this comfortable.

"See his big car sef," he hissed.

****

Back on his bed as he reminisced, he knew he had to make a choice and fast. And then, it occurred to him.

"All this park people sef, those pastors, do they have two heads? And they make a lot of change from passengers...hmmm," smiled, rubbing his jaw in accomplishment. "I will be a man of god!"

He jumped off his bed, wearing a worn out blue shirt and a worn out jean he dashed out of the house with no idea of where his ministry will begin. Taking a walk down the streets and corners of Tudun Wada, he eventually finds himself in front of a motor park, an upcoming motor park "The safe way". He smiled at his new discovery, and observing the men in search of customers, he realized how few they were and they certainly needed a helping hand. Without them asking, he plays his part, "Abuja! Abuja!! Abuja!!!" he yelled, sounding more audible than the three men in search of passengers. And while these three men awed at this audacious fellow they were more surprised when passengers were taking heed and coming towards their vehicle. Tunji adopted the customer-friendly attitude, helping passengers carry their luggage to the car and whispering compliments. These three men sat with their arms folded as they watched Tunji steal the limelight. One of the men wanted to caution Tunji but, the other two insisted he let things be. In three hours, they had three vehicles filled with passengers, a scenario they had never encountered since they opened the motor park a month ago. The men found themselves grateful to Tunji.

"Bro! Thank you ooo! Wetin be your name?!"

Tunji feeling accomplished replied" Tunji-o Bros."

They all laughed together until one of them suggested "Tunji, how we go pay you na, make we sort you small thing?!"

Tunji felt too ambitious for a small thing, he knew he wanted more and this would be a perfect place to begin his ministry.

"Oga! Una get pastor for this park?!" He asked.

"No-o," one of the men replied. "I for like be your pastor for this park. And maybe your boy, make I dey help una pack things for passengers."

The men saw it as a good deal.

"We go tell our Oga at the top, but before that time, you can begin."

Tunji was so elated at the opportunity that without

restriction he rushed to one of the vehicles and started praying for the passengers.

"My people can I get your attention please!"

The passengers went silent to listen.

"Thank you. Praise the Lord!" he shouted with the crowd replying "Alleluia!"

"Brothers and sisters I can't hear you, I said praise the lord!!!"

"Alleluia," they resounded.

"My brothers and sisters in the Lord. I am Pastor Tunji and I am here to tell you about the fear of God. As you are travelling, we need to know that there are obstacles on the way, there are demons on the way. In fact Satan may have planted something evil for you today but I tell you it will be removed in Jesus name!"

And the passengers yelled "Amen!,"

"*Shikaraka bababa shikushikuku*," he babbles. "I have prayed for you, and I know the Lord will take you there safely, in Jesus name!"

"Amen!" they cheered.

"And so people, it is unfair to leave the man of god penniless. Like the Christians of old contributed to the ministry, contribute to the ministry of the man of god, contribute I tell you!" he emphasises, perspiring as he closes his eyes.

The passengers are carried away with everyone pushing their hands into their pockets and purses and saying "God bless you pastor!" Tunji wears a grin as he collects heartily and responds with "God bless you too." The same routine he applied for the second and third vehicles and eventually, when the cars left, he ran to a corner and counted the money he had made. He kept watching out for any one coming close while he counted his fifties and twenties and tens. He had made two thousand naira from offertory. He jumped in excitement and fulfilment, yelling" na God win, na God win, na God win-o" he danced, wagging his bottom like a Yoruba woman, his tall frame made it hilarious. The three fellows, Raymos, Uwa and Ife watched from a distance as he displayed, conscious of what he had done, they had no issues with it.

Tunji's life had taken a new turn. He knew his activity had to come with better packaging and a sweet tongue. He was getting popular in The Safe Way Park. Passengers even asked of him whenever he wasn't available, his name was now Pastor T.J. "Aaah! *Oga* Ife, where is Pastor TJ today, won't anyone pray for us?" asked a passenger when on one occasion Tunji was on an errand.

As the Park was getting popular so was Tunji in his small venture. He was beginning to enjoy the fame and the fact that many were receptive of him. He had learned to smile more and say the words in reference to the Bible. He bought a used six inched television for the sole purpose of watching sermons to improve on his approach. His life was slowly changing, at least he could return home with five hundred naira or more.

Five years, still in the business and he felt he would not

rather be anywhere else. But then, typical of human nature, passengers were slowly beginning to withdraw coupled with the state of the economy. On one occasion while he preached to passengers before the vehicle left, the passengers were virtually deaf to his words; "People of God!" he said,"we don't know how we are going to die! But I tell you that for those who hold on to his mercies nothing shall come their way! Nothing shall befall you! The response he got was lukewarm as many had their heads and minds in different directions but, he still had the zeal to continue.

"Can I hear an Amen people?!"

"Amen" responded a few voices.

"I wish you a safe journey o! But, people, put something down for the man of god...for the progress of the ministry."

On this occasion, he seemed not to have reached out to anyone, he felt he was jinxed because from the offertory he made just fifty naira from two vehicles. Do the people now realize that he is a fake? But he is not fake, he intends being a pastor someday. That night when he returned home, he thought of the events of the day and wondered *how do I get my pride back? Am not a begger o, God forbid!*" He was beginning to feel disrespected and rejected, Tunji felt like showing another part of him, certainly, not the religious one.

Tunji's arrogance was way ahead of him, reminding himself that he was not a beggar and "na condition dey make cray fish bend." This time, humility would not control him, he had to make his money. And so one morning when he could not take being ignored by passengers, he decided to use a passenger as a scapegoat. In his insight, he decided to observe on who is still fervent in dropping offertory, and in his observation, knowing that a particular passenger will not be there on a daily basis, he realized that a good number were beginning to shun him. A certain lady known as Madame-look-good was his first. Unfortunately, she decided to take the Safe Way bus to Abuja one Sunday morning, and while Tunji was preaching to the passengers after loading, Madame-look-good was asking for directions from a fellow passenger on the right route to take to Nyanya in Abuja. Tunji unconsciously in disgust yelled at her "Madame! Won't you wait till you get there? All this talk for here!"

Madame-look-good was too perplexed to reply. She wondered when the familiarity began. Tunji, on the other hand, saw nothing wrong with what he had done. he hissed and lifted his nose in disgust and had the air of " I am not a beggar-o." Every other passenger was surprised at this new character in this jovial fellow or better yet "a man of god!" Despite what was on people's minds, Tunji had a different perception and he was ready to face the consequences not knowing how they'll come.

From that day onward, passengers did not drop a dime or a nickel in his offertory bowl. No one asked after him either. Being at the park daily made Tunji's days frustrating, like heaps of hot coal on his head. But it was too late for him, arrogance had got in the way.

He was invisible to the public after that display to Madame-look-good. Like wild fire, it seems the news spread into the ears of every passenger that patronized the Safe Way Park. His regular pennies become nothing, nothing to own any more.

What kind of life is this? he thought. Looking at all in ire, *"don't they pity my condition?"* Tunji forgot that the world is for the fittest. He knew he had to adapt an aggressive strategy, and fast! And so Tunji made up his mind, unconsciously disgusted by everyone, with a plan no one could fathom. A plan to be achieved in this same park, a plan he must execute. That plan was real but...you don't want to know what next he did.

A Journey

6 a.m. was my timing. I woke up at 7.am instead, truly late to take the first bus to Benin from Jos. Working with 'African time' felt convenient since it's a norm and however early one is, the bus leaves by 11.am or 12.pm thus I found no hurry in taking a shower and eating breakfast. By time I was through with preparations, I left home by 8.am which considerably was early as I was lucky to land the first bus.

The choky buses they have these days and they still extort with conditions of air conditioning which still has conditions. The journey started smoothly and I was fortunate to sit behind the driver close to a window. The window had a way of easing the journey which triggered my excitement and I had no regret working with 'African time'. Besides the air that passes through, one gets a glimpse of the priceless exhibitions of nature for twelve straight hours, certainly a long time to cope with short naps that hurt the neck and the body, but... improvisation is one out of my many skills.

The bus contained over twelve passengers including the driver, plus an Alsatian locked in its cage with whom we shared a seat and some chickens at the back seat tied between a bag of potatoes and tomatoes. Poor animals, I could only imagine the suffocation and frustration they were undergoing and the possible thoughts they incurred like *O humans! What can we do to make you love us?*

The repulsive smell of the perishable foods and domestic animals reminded me of the definition of putrid and I wondered how far will this journey go? I wondered why Africans can't help themselves with so many pieces of luggage and transporting food, especially perishable items, that could be gotten anywhere! So much for considering your fellow man, causing discomfort all through the journey. Suddenly, a woman at the back seat whom I am sure owns the chickens advocated we pray.

"My people-o! E no make sense if we no commit this journey into God hand."

Everyone responded "hmmm..."

"And so," she continued, "in Jesus name!"

"Amen," they responded, with little or no enthusiasm. "I said...in Jesus name!" she emphasized, and they all screamed "Amen!" acknowledging that she won't stop if the response was not resounding. Then, she said the prayer. I honestly do not remember the words but I know it was close to 15 minutes of repetition of the same lines of prayer. My father was calling me persistently, knowing his person, I was so sure he thought I was in an accident or probably my phone was stolen. I could not pick the call since my conscience wouldn't let me and I would disrupt the prayers. I grumbled in my mind and the face I wore could squeeze an orange. As soon as the prayer was over, I sighed in relief and called my parents to explain my case, my father had to ask "na how many hours dem dey take pray?" and I chuckled just to avoid further questions to come.

The driver was quite young, moving at a fast pace, listening to afro-pop music and whistling along, inadvertently interrupting my music which I had plugged to my ears.

Everyone on the bus seemed to be quiet except the driver, moving his steering to his rhythm and drumming to the instrumentals on the wheels.

Travelling felt knew almost every time, with the view of people starting their day early, selling bread and vegetables to travellers and capturing the sight of nature's exuberance of rocks and green fields. I was in deep admiration when our bus abruptly stopped at Riyom, along a bush part and then a female passenger was agitating the driver opens the door in a hurry. I pulled out my ear plugs to ask the man beside me what the issue was.

"Na piss-o!"

In my thoughts all I could say was *women*.

The driver was so pissed.

"Madame, why you no piss before you enter this bus, eh?!" he yelled while he came down from the driver's seat.

"Abeg, make una no vex abeg. I be woman na, eh!" the poor woman looked so pitiful as she apologized and I was so sure her wrapper was about to fall off.

The driver grumbled as he dropped the luggage arranged at the entrance of the bus, over ten ecolac boxes and a bag of rice which supported the boxes. The lady was virtually dancing while she waited for the driver to offload. As soon as she found an opening she jumped out. Lucky her, she was skinny.

The driver leaned on the bus anxiously waiting, the jolly fellow turned grumbler with his arms folded, tapping his foot. Other passengers decided to stretch their feet as the lady was taking forever to come out. The scene pulled my attention as I forgot to plug in my ear plugs, wanting to see the end of it. Hurriedly, the lady dashed out of the bush, swiftly tying her wrapper and shouting "abeg una o… abeg no vex" as she approached the bus. Everyone returned to bus but the driver seemed to have bottled up anger when he had to express himself.

"Madame, abeg next time you wan travel, piss before you enter bus. Na beg I dey beg you so," he said while he rearranged the luggage.

The lady lacked words but she just had to say something

"But…*Oga*, na nature na, eh?"

"Which kind nature?" he retorted. "Which kind nature I ask you? Riyom and Jos far? If na Keffi you wan piss I go understand. No be *nananana* you suppose do-am. If anybody wan piss, now is the right time because I no go stop until we reach Lokoja."

"Aaa… driver!" they all protested

"*Oya* na, let's wait and see," he threatened with his southern accent, while he kept struggling with the ecolac boxes and the bag of rice in a bid to lock the door. The poor fellow, sweating profusely and panting while he tried to close the door which he eventually succeeded in.

I was overwhelmed by the silence of the dog and chickens, seems they sensed intimidation and catastrophe if they had made a sound.

The speeding rate of the driver made my heart skip. Before we could toss and turn we were already in Nasarawa! I must confess, I enjoyed the speed and the loud music from the driver's deck except for certain old women at the back seats, grumbling and protesting although inaudible to the driver since he had loud music.

"Dis boy wan kill us," a lady with a croaky voice said, disgusted and helpless.

"I tell you…is it music or the speed? God help us-o! I just want to see my son," the other added.

I had laughter in my throat, which almost betrayed me. With every turn, we moved like flash and someone made it a duty to scream "Jesus!". Others screamed "driver! Take it easy."

He seemed not to give ear. I felt like the loud music was intentional.

Along the way, we came across a herdsman with his herd of cattle who blocked the entire road causing a hold up for over thirty minutes. Many were afraid to come down from their cars and buses and kept screaming at the herdsman *"wawa! Ka cire su mayun ka nan!"* (fool, move away this witches/wizards of yours) and the herdsman seemed to have cared less as he took his time to guide his herd off the road. Heat was building up and tension was rising and unfortunately, there were no men of the law to caution the herdsman. And so a fellow, who felt he was bold enough, came down from his vehicle to approach the herdsman. As he walked towards him, he looked like he was spitting out curses to the herdsman who stared, looking obviously very angry and then, we heard him whistle, then mumble some words. Suddenly, two cows out of his herd responded to his words and then we saw them dust their hoofs for starters, mooing out loud and instead of the fellow to have observed these signs and changes, he still stood with his hands akimbo as though he was prepared for a bull fight. And then the chase began. I have never seen animals pursue someone with so much vengeance. The poor fellow shouted "Help me ooo! Mummy!!". We were all certain that the fellow was sure to die. We all screamed and many came down to plead with the herdsman. It was so provoking, for me. I wished at that moment the law officers were available but they seem never to be available when you need them. People begged the herdsman and I was amazed at the air he carried, one of so much importance, at the moment. Casually, the herdsman whistled and then we saw the cows halt in a brake and stop their pursuit.

****

Fear may have grasped the dog, as it excreted and vomited simultaneously. Its owner, a stout man, certainly with looks of a dog trainer, seemed to be asleep when a lady behind tapped him.

"Bros, your dog don shit-o! abeg, do something."

The lady was so abrupt but I doubt he cared cause he seemed lost.

"Bingo! Bingo … what is this na, eh?" sounding frustrated with his thick Igbo accent, "shit and piss together, eh Bingo?"

Poor dog! I doubt it could translate but its faeces stank and the driver seemed to have ignored everyone. The man could not ask for him to stop the bus, instead he used paper bags to pack whatever he could clear and disposed of it.

The chickens were no different. They startled at every turn causing a fiasco in combination with the loud music. They flapped their wings, chirped and crowed whenever the bags of potatoes and tomatoes collided on them. The noise was unbearable, we all started complaining.

"Madame, control your chickens!"

She seemed to understand as she waved an apology while she struggled to placate the chickens. I am sure she thought, *how I go tie their mouth?*

Despite the stench and heat, with every passenger putting out their heads through the windows due to the dog's faeces and vomit, I concurred with the driver when everyone was cursing and calling him wicked because he refused to stop the bus for the dog owner to properly clean the cage. The driver ignored all, whistling to his rhythm. Luckily, we got to Lokoja in time for the dog owner to relieve us of our misery and the chickens to be made still and certainly for the driver to maintain silence. I must admit, I was getting tired of the noise. I cherished silence in its briefness. We stopped at a fast food restaurant and everyone alighted as soon as the driver offloaded, those same grumbling individuals did not confront the "enemy" when they looked him in the face.

We all had a meal except for the dog owner who spent his restricted ten minutes cleaning the dog and its cage. I felt bad for him but then I wondered why so much stress in transporting the animal if it's inconvenient. But then I remembered "the cheaper, the better."

Ten minutes was exact with the driver already awaiting passengers to enter the bus.

"Abeg o! The people wey dey dis bus...make una come-o!"

We all entered the bus and the driver arranged the luggage and easier and quicker this time. Probably he was hungry earlier. Immediately he locked the door, he walked swiftly round and jumped into the driver's seat, turned the ignition key, made a fast turn and the speed continued.

It was a peaceful journey, despite the fast speed. The dog and the chickens seemed accustomed to the situation, except for the grumbling women who complained at every bump. Once we passed Okene in Kogi State, we encountered another hold-up, but this time it was a cultural display of masquerades dressed in different colours parading along the roads. The masquerades had followers trailing behind them and seemed to scare anyone who came their way. A passenger in the bus said "their eye no suppose see woman-o." But I saw the contrary cause a crowd of both men and women were intrigued by the acts of the masquerade and the music that played.

Thankfully, we passed that scene and while on our way still within Okene along a wild bush path, the driver said out loudly "Na here dem rob us yesterday." Every woman in the bus (except myself) screamed " blood of Jesus!" I think one of the ladies spat *"tufai!"* All I could think of was so much for exaggeration. Yulk!

We then came across a ghastly motor accident which took place along the same way between a Lamborghini and a trailer. The women in the bus could not just hide their emotions. I am sure if God judged based on the way we profess his name in vain those ladies would have had a clean ticket to hell. Suddenly, there was a new session of prayers and then another lady screamed at the driver.

"Driver! You no go learn from the accident... eh?! We will not die like this in Jesus name!"

"Amen," they all replied.

The dog seemed to have concurred as it replied with a "whoof!"

Eventually, we entered Edo State and a passenger alighted, luckily, it was the lady with the chickens. One stench off!

While we drove ahead, we came across a passenger heading for Benin whom the driver picked. I have never met a man who talked so repulsively, rambling about sports and politics to women who were only concerned about their safety. At that moment, my ear plugs were an asset. As we were closing in on Benin, the driver decided to make a stop at a stable for dry gin. He jumped out of the vehicle, and obvious to all eyes he gulped two shots.

The women in the bus went haywire.

"God-o!" exclaimed one,

"I know your face-o! I will never enter this bus again!" another threatened.

And the others kept murmuring.

I almost tumbled with laughter.

As for the driver, he ignored the crowd, hopped into the vehicle and before we knew it, we were in the park, the final stop.

Everyone came out of the bus slowly, a few stretching and others praising God for a rugged journey. I even overheard a woman say "thank God, I go see my pickin. Hmmm," she sighed in relief.

The cab men were available for hire and they were booked almost immediately. The guy with the dog decided to hire one and in a bid to release the dog to stretch its feet, the dog seized the opportunity to run wild. It ran fast and wide with the owner screaming "Bingo! Bingo!!" The dog was up for a chase and I think an escape.

Well, I stepped out of the vehicle with no friend or issue but truly satisfied with the comical events that played. But I certainly thought of how to make it home.

I wouldn't have had it any other way. Thumbs up to the driver and, most of all, Thank God for a safe ride!

Printed in the United States
By Bookmasters